SAVAGE ENDING

NEW YORK TIMES BESTSELLING AUTHOR
LISA RENEE JONES

ISBN-13: 979-8500553171

www.lisareneejones.com

BE THE FIRST TO KNOW!

The best way to be informed of all upcoming books, sales, giveaways, televisions news (there's some coming soon!), and to get a FREE EBOOK, be sure you're signed up for my newsletter list!

SIGN-UP HERE: http://lisareneejones.com/newsletter-sign-up/

Another surefire way to be in the know is to follow me on BookBub:

FOLLOW ME HERE: http://bookbub.com/authors/lisa-renee-jones

CHARACTERS

Candace Marks— long dark hair, green eyes. Architect. Father (Howard Marks) is a general in the army, her mother was an officer in the army, but died in an accident on duty. She fell in love with Rick Savage eight years ago, before he left and broke her heart.

Rick Savage—dark hair, deep blue eyes, six-foot-five. Former surgical resident and green beret. Lives in NYC, works for Walker Security. Father was a surgeon, mother is deceased. Scar on his cheek. Goatee. Tattoos: a skull in a Green Beret, a snake, and a knife on his chest, a heart that says San Antonio. Gave his heart to Candace, and left it with her when he joined the black ops team. Now he's back to settle a score and get his woman back.

Tag—led the missions Savage went on when he was a mercenary. Smoker. Father-like figure to Savage until he found out the truth. Killed in *Savage Love*.

Savage's father—thick solid gray hair, thin frame. Alcoholic. Was horrible to his wife, yelled and shoved her, she had a heart attack and died—Candace was a witness. Is in rehab.

Howard Marks—Five-Star General. Pulled Savage into the black ops team eight years ago. Was saved by Walker Security when Tag threatened to kill him.

Linda—pretty, petite, blonde. Candace's best friend. Owns a floral shop.

Max—part of Savage's black ops team. His wife, Kelly, called Savage in a panic because he's missing. Savage arranged for Walker Security to get to Kelly so she'd be safe while he looks into Max's disappearance. Kelly ended up ditching Walker Security and went to find Max on her own.

Adam—former Navy SEAL Team Six. Walker Security employee. Tall and broad, dark hair.

Smith—former Army Ranger, Walker Security employee. Sandy brown hair.

Blake Walker—Savage's boss at Walker Security. One of the founding brothers. Has been helping remotely.

Kara Walker—Married to Blake. Part of Walker Security.

Asher—former Navy SEAL Team Six. Walker Security employee. Hacker. Rockstar looks—long blond hair, tattoos.

Adrian Mack—Tall, dark, and good-looking with curly dark hair. Brown eyes. Friendly. Ex-FBI. Lots of tattoos. Walker Security employee. Savage is unsure of him.

Royce Walker—Eldest brother of the founding Walker Security brothers. Married to Lauren.

Lauren Walker— Attorney. Married to Royce.

Luke Walker—The middle brother of the founding Walker Security brothers. Married to Julie.

Julie Walker— Attorney. Married to Luke.

CHAPTER ONE

Savage

Candace and I exit Jimmy's Pancakes and Burgers, into a crisp New York City October morning.

"I don't know Jimmy, or why Jimmy loves Pancakes and Burgers, but he's a brilliant chef," I say.

"Somehow I doubt Jimmy is a chef," she laughs, catching my arm. "And Jimmy wasn't here today."

"He created the recipes. He trained the staff. And after a breakfast of champions that includes waffles, pancakes, bacon, sausage, and egg whites—gotta be healthy—I'm not sure how you can insult Jimmy that way. He's Top Chef material. This is going to be our new Saturday morning spot."

I guide her onto the busy sidewalk, and there is no question my little sugar plum of a bride-to-be is looking delicious herself in an emerald green sweater, dress slacks, and a Burberry trenchcoat. I, on the other hand, am in the uniform of the gods: jeans and a long-sleeved T-shirt, at the sugar plum's request—a nice one at that without any dirty slogans on it—and boots. The leather jacket was her idea, as well.

We round a corner and Candace squeezes my arm, pointing at the imposing masterpiece of two towers ahead of us, which also happens to be our destination. And of course, the location of the meeting that had her changing her clothes over and over this morning. "There it is!" she proclaims. "It's so incredibly gorgeous. I *cannot believe* Blake arranged for us to be married in St. Patrick's cathedral. Well, if the priest approves our wedding. Today will tell all. But I mean, when we decided to move the wedding here, instead of Texas, I never dreamed this could happen. There's a waitlist *years long.*" She laughs. "I'm rambling. I'm a little excited, if you didn't notice. But coffee with the wedding coordinator went well, don't you think?"

"I wasn't there," I remind her.

She laughs again. "Right. Nerves are getting the best of me. And today is what matters. You'll be with me and we'll talk to the powers that be for a final approval of the wedding. This is it. This is the real deal."

She's so damn excited. She's dreamed of our special day for so long. And I don't want to ruin it for her, but there's a potential problem that's punching at my mind, refusing to be ignored. A big-ass fucking problem. And yet, my baby girl is all but bouncing toward the steps leading up to the doors to the cathedral. The problem being the walk up, and I tell myself I can do this. One step. Two. My feet are lead, but I keep moving up.

We stop at the doors, and I turn to Candace, hands on her shoulders. "I don't know about this, Candy, baby."

She blinks. "What do you mean?"

"Come on. You know who I am. You know *what* I am. I'm marked for the devil. I'm not sure I can walk into that church."

She smiles. "Don't be silly. You're not marked for the devil."

"Candace," I whisper, a plea for her to understand, to see the truth.

She wraps her arms around me and says, "God knows what's in your heart. *I* know what's in your heart."

"You," I say softly. "You are."

"I love you, Rick. Let's go talk to the priest and do the walk-through Friday night."

"What if he—"

"Loves you as much as I do?"

I cup her head, thinking of all the people I've killed. "I think you love me too much. You're blind."

"You're the one who is blind, Rick. You always think you're the devil. And that almost tore us apart."

I cup her head and lean in close. "I am the devil, baby. You just cut my wings."

"Stop it," she orders. "Rick Savage—"

My mouth slants over hers and I kiss her deeply, drink her in, my anger, my salvation, and when I come up for air, I hear, "Save that for the honeymoon, please."

At the sound of a woman's voice, I curse. "Fuck."

Candace laughs. "Ah, my Savage." She pats my chest and glances at the woman. "Rosa. So good to see you again."

I bite back another fuck when I realize I've just made out with my wife-to-be and cursed in front of Madame Judgement, the woman who holds Candace's dreams in her little hand. I eye Rosa, a slight little thing in her sixties, and tilt my chin in her direction. "Sorry about that, ma'am."

Her lips curve. "Nothing wrong with being human and your recovery is quite polite. I like that in a husband-to-be." She motions toward the church. "Let's go inside and chat with the priest. Oh, and Candace, how would a March wedding sound to you?"

Candace's eyes light up. "That would be wonderful."

"That is forever from now," I interject. "I've waited a long time to marry her. Can we do this any faster?"

"Eagerness is appreciated," Rosa states, "but she's running to you, not away. You have a lifetime together."

Candace captures my hand in hers. "Yes, we do," she says softly.

Rosa offers an approving look and motions us forward. She disappears inside the church and when Candace would step forward, I tug her toward me. "Five months is too long to wait."

She studies me for a moment and presses her hand to my face. "We don't have to do this here or in March. I love you. I don't need this. I need *you*. But we're still walking into the church."

I blink. "What? Why?"

"Because you're afraid of yourself and therefore this church. You have to get over that. You're not going to burn up or be struck with lightning when you enter."

"That's up for debate and possibly not for long."

"We're going inside, Rick," she says sternly. "And then we'll decide when and where to get married, over a drink I believe you need right now."

She steps inside the church and tugs me forward. Of course, I could hold my ground, but damn it, she's right. I'm *afraid*. Which is embarrassing. Rick fucking Savage is not a pussy-ass bitch scaredy-cat. I hold my breath, steel myself for what may happen next, and follow her inside the church. I don't burn up. Lightning doesn't strike me down. "Thank you, God," I murmur.

Candace steps in front of me and smiles. "See? All is well." Her gaze lifts to the towering ceiling painted with biblical images and she murmurs, "Incredible." She twists in my arms and stares at the giant pillars attached by towering arches that frame the rows of seats, stained glass in every arched window, of which there are many.

Rosa steps next to Candace. "It's stunning, isn't it?"

"Yes," she whispers. "It really is that and more."

I imagine Candace walking down the aisle. This is a place of a Cinderella storybook wedding. And after all she's been through, after all I put her through, she deserves a Cinderella story of her own.

This is where we're getting married.

Candace turns to look at me and when her eyes meet mine, she reads my mind and grants me a perfect, beautiful smile. The kind that lights up a room and this dark heart of mine. She throws her arms around me, fixing me in a pretty green stare, love in her eyes. "We're getting married right here."

I stroke hair. "Yes," I say. "We are. Forever and ever, baby."

"Forever and ever," she agrees.

"Shall we?" Rosa queries, directing us to our left. "The priest is waiting on us."

"As long as he's willing to marry a sinner and an angel," I say. "Lead the way."

A few minutes later, after Rosa meets with the priest one on one, we're brought into an office lined with books. The priest, a man in his sixties, with white hair, but a young voice and chiseled face, studies us from behind a heavy wooden desk. "Who's the sinner and who's the angel?"

"I'm the sinner," I say. "Is that a problem?"

"It's not my role to judge you," the priest assures me. "But you're welcome to join me in the confession booth."

"No," Candace says quickly. "That won't be necessary."

I laugh and she scowls at me.

"That won't be necessary," I repeat. "We wouldn't want to scare you away, Father."

He laughs, and says, "I don't scare easily, but let's move on and talk about your wedding."

And just like that, I dodge the confession booth and a bullet.

We're home-free and walking with fancy feet now.

Onward to the wedding.

And the hot honeymoon night.

LISA RENEE JONES

CHAPTER TWO

$\mathcal{S}$avage

March, less than a week before the wedding...

"Is Barney getting married and why are you showing me his purple tuxedo?"

The store attendant, some new guy who has his nose in the air and a stick up his ass, bristles. "Is this not your tuxedo?"

Adam laughs. "Can it please be his tuxedo?"

I scowl in his direction and then eye the snobby attendant with a badge that reads "Nicolas." He is such a fucking Nicolas, too, which as far as I'm concerned is the equivalent to a Karen. Nicolas scowls. "The tag says right here, Jackie Mitchell. If you have buyer's remorse—"

"Once upon a time Jackie and Jill went up the hill. If I were Jackie, Jill would tumble right on top of me and stay there. But I am not, in fact, Jackie. If I *was* Jackie, I'd give someone a gun and tell them to shoot me."

Nicolas blinks at me. "You're not Jackie?"

"Jesus," Adam murmurs. "No. He is *not* Jackie."

"Oh," Nicolas states. "Well then, what is your name?"

"Rick Savage and they call me Savage for a reason, Nicolas. Take the purple tuxedo to Barney."

He purses his lips and without so much as an apology, he walks away. I eye Adam and plop onto a velvet high back chair across from him. "I'm a cranky bitch, right?"

"You are a cranky bitch," Adam confirms, "but he deserves it. He has crap customer service skills. And you're the customer, the groom, who's nervous as fuck."

"I am," I admit, scrubbing my jaw. "I just don't want to screw up with Candace, you know?"

"Candace knows what she's getting herself into. She's not going anywhere."

My cellphone rings and I snatch it from my pocket to find an unknown caller. My Spidey senses tingle. Spidey senses never mean anything good is about to happen. I answer the call with a scowl. "Who is this?"

"Max. It's Max, Savage."

And there it is. A problem. A piece of my past, a man I worked with under Tag. A man I killed with, and survived with, for all the wrong reasons. "Why are you calling?"

"You owe me."

He's talking about saving my life. I turn away from Adam. "Debt paid," I remind him softly and add, "Times two." I'm referencing Walker protecting his wife when he was on the run from Tag, when Tag would have killed him and her, alike. I also killed Tag and solved that problem for him.

"Iraq, Mexico, Washington," he says. "Three debts. Two down. One to go."

I curse because he's right. He saved my ass three fucking times. I walk down the hallway and exit to the alleyway. "What do you want?"

"I wasn't just hiding from Tag. I made an enemy. A bad enemy."

I go cold, the promises I've made to Candace about who, and what, I am, playing in my head. "You want me to kill him."

"You won't have to," he assures me. "I have a data drive. If you get it to the right person, he'll kill him for me. Just deliver the data. Debt paid."

"What's on the drive?"

"It's better you don't know."

"I need to know."

SAVAGE ENDING

"No," he says. "No, you do not. But if this doesn't happen soon, me and my wife, we're dead. He's closing in on us. I feel it. And I'm running out of money."

"I know how much money you made because I was right there with you making it. You're rolling in bucks."

"And getting to it is risky. You know how that is. I burned through my cash. I'm texting you the pick-up and drop-off details now. Pick-up is at a cabin in Gatlinburg and drop-off about three hours down the road. Call me when you get to Tennessee."

"Who am I picking up from?"

"No one involved in any of this. It's complicated, but not messy."

"All right," I say. "I can bring you some cash after I deliver. Where are you?"

"You could lead that bastard to me."

I snort at that. "Come the fuck on, man. This is me you're talking about. And if this bastard, whoever he is, finds me, I'll kill him. Which is why you need to tell me who he is."

His rejection is hard and fast. "I'm not pulling you into this. Just in and out, nice and clean. Invisible."

I want to push for more, but a cellphone isn't a safe way to extract information. "Where are you?" I repeat. "I'll bring you money and we can drink to this being over for you and me."

He hesitates and then says, "I'm texting the address. Thanks, man. If you pull this off, the story reverses. I owe you."

"No debt. I'm done after this." I disconnect and slide my phone back in my pocket, wondering how the fuck I'm going to tell Candace I'm leaving days before our wedding.

My phone buzzes with a text, and I glance down to read the locations Max has sent me. I'm headed to Tennessee and then Colorado. I text the private airport Walker frequents and put a plane on hold.

Once that's done, I walk back inside the building to find Adam's big-ass self waiting in the hallway. "What was that?"

"You aren't my mother, man. Back up."

15

"But I'm your damn brother from another mother. What the fuck was that?"

He's right. He is my brother from another mother, which is exactly why I don't lie to him. And I'm not getting him involved in my bullshit. I blow past him and bump the fuck out of his shoulder as I walk on by him. Because what's a brother for if not to show love?

Nicolas is waiting on me. "Your tuxedo is missing," he announces.

I decide right then the universe is conspiring to keep me away from Candace, but it won't work. If I have to show up to the church in my birthday suit, the way God brought me into this world, I will. Nothing will keep me from marrying my baby girl.

CHAPTER THREE

Candace

Less than one week.

In less than one week, I will finally marry the love of my life.

I stand on a pedestal in the center of the bridal shop's dressing room and stare at myself in the mirror. My dress is ivory, with a plunging neckline, but the sheer flesh-colored mesh neckline somehow defines it as less daring than it truly is. And the back, the back is stunning, low cut with the same mesh.

"The flowers down the skirt and train are just stunning," Julie exclaims.

Julie is the blonde bombshell wife of Luke Walker, the middle Walker brother who I've spent the last six months getting to know. Her and Lauren, Royce Walker's wife, have become fast friends who have made New York City feel like home. Julie is also pale and a little sickly today, having just found out that she's pregnant. "I pray I don't get sick at your wedding," Julie says, turning paler and sitting down on a bench.

"If you do," I declare, "we'll make the men clean it up."

She laughs. "That would be entertaining." She glances at her watch. "Grrr. I have to get to a meeting. Lauren and I have a new client. Someone Royce really wants us to take on."

Lauren and Julie are the lawyers who support Walker's clients. It's really amazing, I think, the way the Walker team has created a circle of work, family, and friends. And now

I'm a part of that circle. Well, not the work part. I design buildings, so I'm not exactly their go-to person for Walker cases. But a Walker clan of about thirty did surprise me with gallons of ice cream and champagne to help me celebrate a contract to design a new apartment by the Hudson River.

Julie pushes to her feet. "I'd hug you, but I'm not going to risk messing up that dress. It's gorgeous and you're gorgeous. And wear your hair down. It's such a shiny dark brown, it's luscious."

"Lucious?" I snicker. "My hair is *luscious*?"

"You know it, darlin'." She blows me a kiss and rushes away, "Call me tonight!"

"I will," I promise over my shoulder, a smile on my lips. "How are we doing, Candace?"

My gaze roams to the doorway where Mary, my seamstress, a pretty brunette with lush dark curls, has rejoined us. "Fabulous," I say. "Thank you. I think those small adjustments you made last fitting were needed."

"Excellent." She clasps her fingers together and gives me and my dress an inquiring eye. "I do need to pin a couple of spots here and there for a few more tiny adjustments. I know you say it's perfect, but it's not quite there yet. Give me a few more minutes, if you can? It's insanity in here today and I want to be focused to make your final adjustments."

"I don't mind leaving it on just a little longer one bit," I assure her. "Take your time."

She smiles a knowing smile, well versed on brides who are enamored with their own dresses. "Let me detach your train so you can sit," she suggests, and quickly moves behind me, removes the attachment, and then hangs it up. "Now you can enjoy champagne." She fills a glass and sets it on a table in the corner, near two comfy chairs. "I'll hurry back," she promises.

She rushes away and I rotate to the mirror, quickly noting the fact that my pale skin is glowing and why would it not be? I'm marrying Rick Savage. After all those years apart from him, all those painful years, we're together. The rear door opens and closes, and I assume it's a staff member or a delivery. My attention is back on the gown, but I'm thinking about Rick. He'd been awkward with the priest, but so very Savage.

"I'll just be frank, Father," Rick says, after we sit down across from the priest in his office, and right after we've been told the priest is the final say in who does and does not get married in the church. "I'm not what you'd call a good guy, but God didn't strike me down with lightning when I walked in here, so he's made his judgment. I'm with an angel, I'm marrying an angel, and I need her to have her fairytale wedding. Are you going to keep her from having what God clearly wants for her?"

The priest leans forward and smiles. "What God giveth, I cannot taketh away. And for the record, Rick Savage, we're all sinners."

"There are different levels of sin," Savage counters. "I'm the one foot into hell kind of sinner," I take his hand and he adds, "but she pulled me back."

"Sounds like we should visit the confessional before you leave, son."

"God no," I spurt, with my heart racing. "No," I add. "I ah—pardon me, Father. Let's save that for after the wedding."

Savage laughs and to my surprise, so does the priest before he says, "Let's talk about the wedding."

I smile with the memory and with the plans for the wedding.

Married in our new home city, where we have started our new life, a beautiful day, and church, with our new family watching. Of course, my father and a few friends will join us as well. Sadly, Rick's father going into rehab has not mended their relationship. Savage will not invite him to the wedding.

I blink myself back into view and dream of the moment I walk down the aisle wondering how Rick will react.

A whistle lifts in the air and my gaze jerks to the left to find Rick standing in the hallway. Tall, dark, and dangerous—the love of my life who is always a rebel, living outside the rules. He cannot be here. It breaks every rule in the pre-wedding book.

It's bad luck that we do not need.

CHAPTER FOUR

Candace

At the sight of my future husband, staring at me in my wedding dress, I do the only thing I can do.

I fling my arms around myself, attempting to hide any little part of my dress from Rick, who should *not* be here. "You can't see me in my dress!" I shout. "Go, Rick. Go now!" He doesn't go. He's staring at me with his piercing blue eyes, gobbling me up with a hungry look. "You're beautiful, baby. So fucking beautiful."

I twist around, away from him, desperate to find a robe, but it's too late. He's already in front of me, all six-foot-five inches of hot, hard man, dragging me against him. "God, woman." His voice is raspy, affected, and he cups my head and leans in close. "I can't believe you're finally going to be my wife."

Wife.

His wife.

The very idea undoes me and heats my skin and my heart.

My fight and flight mechanisms are both weak as the warmth of his body consumes mine. His eyes are filled with love, and that love is exactly what draws my attention to the scar on his cheek that represents so much of our past. The bad parts that almost took him from me forever. "Rick, damn it," I whisper. "This is bad luck."

"Nothing about you and me is bad luck, baby," he says. "*You* are my lucky charm, woman. Haven't you figured that out?"

My heart softens, and the remainder of my resistance fades away. "I wanted to surprise you on our wedding day." "You surprise me every day of our lives." He strokes hair behind my ear, a tenderness that defies a man who can be brutal to his enemies and kisses me, a soft brush of lips to my lips, before he says, "I love you more than I knew any human being could love. You know that, right?"

"Oh no! Oh my God!" Mary exclaims. "He can't see you before the wedding!"

Rick kisses me again. "Tell her to go away."

"Rick," I hiss. "She's my seamstress. This is her store."

He acts as if she isn't here, and says, "I have to run an errand for an old friend. I'm going to be gone for a few days."

My heart leaps. Rick's old friends are trouble, the kind that gets people killed. I turn to Mary. "Can we have just a minute, Mary, please?"

"This is bad luck," she insists. "I mean, if this is your fiancé."

I'd bristle, but Rick snorts a laugh. "Don't mind me," he says. "I'm just the best man. No bad luck here."

I swat him. "Stop." And then I eye Mary. "This is Rick, Mary. Forgive his bad jokes. Just please give me a moment to kill him in private. I won't leave the body in the store."

She bristles, no laughter for her, and then turns on her heel and disappears out into the store again. I face off with Rick. "What friend?" I demand.

"Max."

"As in Max who was working with for Tag as a mercenary?"

"That would be him," he confirms.

"Tag did bad things. He had you and Max do bad things. I don't trust him."

"In my defense, I thought I was working for your father, an honorable general in the United States Army, and so did Max."

That old history with my father is a rough bump in the road. I love my father, but his role in how, and why, Rick ended up a mercenary is not easy to forgive. For now, I focus on Rick. "Tag tried to kill us. How do you know Max isn't dirty?"

"He was like me. In with Tag for the right reasons and trapped when it turned dirty."

"What does he want you to do?" I ask.

"He needs me to deliver something to a friend. He'd do it, but he's still in hiding."

"Why? Tag is dead. Why can't he come out of hiding like you are?"

"Apparently, he had other enemies."

"And he wants you to make an enemy of that enemy?" I challenge and I don't give him time to reply. "I don't like this, Rick. It's less than a week before our wedding."

"All the more reason for me to put the past behind us."

"No," I say. "Can't he just send someone else to do whatever you're going to do?"

"He doesn't trust anyone else." He cups my face. "He saved my life. Three times, Candace. I owe him one last favor."

"We sheltered his wife from Tag. Walker protected her."

"That counted as two. I owe him one more, baby. I wouldn't be here to marry you if not for him. I'll be gone two days at the most. It's a quick shot South and back."

"South, where?"

"Pick-up in Tennessee and delivery to Colorado."

"What is it that you're delivering?"

He kisses me. "Money and data. He needs some cash."

I can tell I will not win this battle and I say, "Damn it, Rick. Please don't die."

His hand flattens on my back. "I have you to live for, Candace. I will be in that church to marry you."

"Promise."

"On my life, baby. On my life." He brushes his lips over mine. "I'll be home soon." And then he releases me and he's walking away.

I have this clawing feeling that he's never coming back. I can't take it. I can't let this happen.

I have to do something.

Lifting my skirts, I hurry into the private dressing area and dig my phone from my purse. I consider my options and decide Savage's closest friend, Adam, is the right choice. I hit his autodial.

"Candace," he says. "What's up?"

"Rick is going to run some errand for an old friend."

He's quiet a beat before he says, "Who?"

"Max. It's Max and he worked for Tag. You know that's trouble. I'm worried, Adam."

"When?"

"He just left the bridal shop. He said he's going to Tennessee and Colorado. Adam, *I'm worried*," I repeat.

"I'll handle it," he promises, and then he just hangs up.

I want to scream. Can he not say more? Can he not tell me more?

I squeeze my eyes shut and now I pray. "Dear Lord. Please don't take him from me again. I can't survive losing Rick Savage yet again."

CHAPTER FIVE

Savage

I swing by the apartment I now share with Candace, toss some items in a bag, and I'm off to the airport via a hired car. It's not long before I'm at the Walker terminal and I'm cursing to find Adam and Asher already at the boarding door, both with bags on their shoulders.

"You fucker," I growl, aiming my attention at Adam. "She called you, didn't she?"

"Of course, she called me," Adam replies. "She loves you. And I called Asher."

I eye Asher, a complicated dude who was a former lead singer in a rock band, turned badass with a computer and a firearm. "Three's a crowd," I say. "Go home and cuddle with your wife and let her run her fingers through all that long-ass blond hair."

He pats his bag, tats running from his hand to his shoulder beneath his sleeve. "You need my laptop, man, with me operating it."

"You're married," I say. "I'm not going to be the reason you don't go home to your woman."

"If this isn't dangerous, as you told Candace," Adam challenges, "then why would he end up dead?"

"Fuck you, Adam. You can go." I eye Asher. "You cannot."

"My wife is busy helping with the wedding," Asher says. "Your wedding that you have to live to experience. I'm going. And judging from this little conversation, you need me, you hard-headed bastard."

I scowl, scrub my jaw and stalk toward the doors, exiting to a short walk down a few steps. Both the assholes follow me and when I arrive at the jet, Adam is the one who starts chit-chatting with the crew. Fucking Chatty Cathy. I'm going to start calling him that. Chatty fucking-pain-in-my-ass Cathy. He followed me when I went to kill Tag and beg for Candace to take me back. Of course, I didn't know I was going to beg her to take me back, but I should have. Holy hell, just seeing her again undid me in a way I didn't know I could be undone anymore, by anything or anyone.

I claim a seat on the plane and Asher is right there, in a recliner across from me. "All right," he says. "Tell me what you know. We're doing a delivery. To and from where?" He pulls his MacBook from his bag.

On this, I don't argue. Something about this whole delivery and pick-up shit Max is spewing is nagging at me, a fly buzzing around my head I can't seem to swat. I pull out my phone and read him the first address in Gatlinburg, Tennessee. "Beautiful little place," Asher says. "You ever been?"

"Never," I say. "And I couldn't give a shit if it's beautiful."

"Point is, asshole," Asher replies, "I know the town. That might be helpful." He types in the address, and says, "That address says its land is owned by a George Monroe."

Adam sits down next to Asher. "Who the hell is George Monroe?"

"I assume an alias for Max," I say, despite Max's claim otherwise but I'm waiting for Asher's input. That fly is still buzzing around my head.

"If it is," Asher says, "it's a pretty damn elaborate alias. George has worked at the aerial tramway in Gatlinburg for twenty years. But, before that, he *was* military."

"That's a potential connection to Max," Adam says. "Which sounds like a dangerous mistake Max wouldn't make."

"Unless there's no connection to his family at all," I counter.

"If he's using the address," Asher says, punching his keyboard and watching his screen not me, "there's a connection."

Asher continues to type and says, "I don't see a connection." He glances at me. "Where are we delivering?"

"We pick up in Gatlinburg, drop off in Nashville, and then I need to drop off cash to Max in Colorado."

"Nashville?" Adam says. "Why can't the guy in Gatlinburg drop off to Nashville? It's what? Four hours away?"

That fly is buzzing around my head again. Why indeed, I think.

"It feels like a set-up, Savage," Adam says, leaning forward and giving me a worried look.

I'd agree, but this is Max. He has no reason to set me up. We were on the same side. Fuck. Unless we weren't. Unless I have an enemy that's his enemy. Or he needs money and that means helping one of my enemies. My lips press together and I read off the Nashville address to Asher. He keys it in and says, "A restaurant on the strip. Who are you delivering to there?"

"He said to ask for the owner."

"Huh," Asher says as if he doesn't like the gist of the message and the truth is, neither do I. He returns his attention to his MacBook and then quickly says, "Jess Kelly is fifty, and retired military. Opened the restaurant ten years ago." He eyes me. "Ring any bells?"

I shake my head, and he says, "Text me the address in Colorado. Let me see if I can make any connections in the locations." The plane engine roars to life and I text Asher the address in Colorado while he works on more information.

Asher goes to work. Adam changes seats, landing in the one next to me. "I know you trust Max, but something feels off."

That's the problem, I think. I'm not sure I do trust Max, and yet he saved my life. But I was the guy at his back, too. Men that are mercenaries, as we were, are in the moment, satisfying what works for us at the time. I don't really know

Max. And I damn sure don't know what motivates him in the moment.

CHAPTER SIX

Candace

As soon as the fitting is done, I send my hired car on his way and head for the subway, which gets me where I'm going faster than a driver. It took this Texas girl a while to appreciate the subway, but now that I do, I prefer it. A short train ride later, I'm at the residential side of the Walker building, punching in a security code. A quick trek up a few flights of stairs and I'm knocking on Blake and Kara's door.

Blake answers the door, and I blink. His long dark hair is not long anymore. "Who are you and what did you do to Blake?"

He laughs a low deep rumble. "Kara says it gets in the way, so I cut it."

"I'm not going to ask for details," I say. "But I think it looks good. Can I visit with Kara?"

"Kitchen," he says, backing up as I enter their gorgeous, recently remodeled, apartment. The floors are a shiny dark wood. The ceiling is covered in closely linked wood beams, while thicker wood beams support the structure. The kitchen island is made of the same wood as the floors, with a contrasting black flecked countertop. I find Kara behind that island, her dark hair piled on top of her head, and flour all over her face.

"Did you come to save me?" she asks.

I step to the opposite side of the counter as her and study the explosion of powdery substances all over the counter, and a bowl that seems to hold thick dough. "I didn't know you baked?"

"I don't, but Lauren has a big trial and she needs cookies for her kiddo's St. Patrick's Day party and it's not even St. Patrick's Day. I told her I'd help."

"Just order them from a bakery."

"It's for tomorrow."

"The grocery store bakery?"

"I looked," she says. "They're sold out. Apparently, everyone thought of this but me. What was I thinking?" she asks herself, trying to stir the sticky dough. "I'm the one you ask to do a self-defense class, not bake cookies."

I laugh. She's right, she is. She's beautiful and sweet, but oh so tough and just as dangerous as any man on the Walker team. She's a rock star.

"Slice and bake is an option," I say, eyeing her work in progress. "Because what you have in that bowl is not edible."

She stops fussing with the dough and eyes me. "Slice and bake. You're brilliant." She calls out, "Blake!"

He appears almost instantly and she gives him a pleading look. "Can you go grab slice and bake cookies?"

"If it will end this baking nightmare, hell yes."

"And icing," I say, glancing at Kara. "Unless you have icing?"

"I have a recipe," she offers.

"The cookie icing is best," I say, "but cake icing will work if needed."

Like the devoted husband he is, Blake rushes for the door.

Kara sets the bowl in the sink. "I didn't know you baked."

"I fake bake. My mother was an officer in the Army. Baking wasn't her priority." I quickly change the subject. "Kara, I need to know about Max and Kelly."

She grabs a napkin and wipes her hands. "I don't know them at all. I mean, Kelly stayed with me a few days when Max was missing, but she took off to find Max. Why? Are you inviting them to the wedding?"

"No," I say, and pause because that's a reality here I hadn't thought of before now. Max and Kelly weren't invited to the wedding. If Savage called Max a true friend, they would be. "No, but Savage just took off to do a favor for Max."

She frowns. "What kind of favor?"

"He said a pick-up and drop-off. Something to do with someone hunting Max and Max can't do it."

She tosses the napkin down. "Right before the wedding? And I didn't know they were that great of friends. That is something we do for our inner circle."

"They aren't," I say. "But Savage says Max saved his life. I called Adam. He was going to 'handle it,' he said. I don't know what that means."

"It means the dumbass loyal beast of a man of yours isn't alone. Adam wouldn't let him go alone. Let's drink wine and wait on Blake. He'll get to the bottom of this."

I sigh and give a tiny nod, but while she heads to the bar for the wine, I reach for my phone and walk to the floor-to-ceiling windows in their living room, where I dial Savage. He doesn't answer. I dial Adam next. He too doesn't answer.

Kara appears and hands me a glass. "Anything?"

"No," I say. "I assume they're both on a plane."

"I texted with Blake. He says Savage, like the rest of the guys, pay for personal use of the planes. He booked a flight into Tennessee and then to Colorado and then back here. Blake assumed he was taking you somewhere."

The doorbell rings. "I'll be right back," Kara says, hurrying to greet her visitor.

I stare out the window, without seeing the Hudson river below, trying to be comforted by the fact that Savage's route matches what he told me. But why wouldn't it? He doesn't lie to me. Savage told me the truth, and nothing but the truth. In other words, he doesn't really know what he's getting himself into. Of that I'm certain.

I consider calling my father, who'd been the entire reason Savage had gotten involved with Tag. Savage wanted to please him, but no, I'm not risking my father making a call, or poking the wrong bear, that turns attention onto Savage. My father got in too deep with Tag as well, and saw friends where there were enemies. These war games get dangerous and dirty quickly.

At the sound of voices, I turn to find Sierra, Asher's wife, with Kara. I know without being told that Asher went with Adam and Savage. And I tell myself that with a team of three Walker warriors on the case, nothing can go wrong.

Savage will be back home soon.

Safe.

And then we'll get married.

I down my glass of wine, and will it to make me stop thinking of Tag, and Max's connection to that monster. I will myself to stop thinking of everything that could go wrong.

CHAPTER SEVEN

Savage

We lift off at four o'clock, with a three-hour flight ahead of us, landing at a small strip an hour from our destination, which suits me fine. Darkness does a man right when he wants to live and love the woman he's about to marry. And other dirty things he already knows said wifey-to-be will not only agree to but enjoy.

As for Asher and Adam, they're both asleep, out of the necessity of an upcoming night mission, while I'm not. I'm thinking about Candace, who I should be holding, or fucking, or loving, and just talking to right now. But I know she knows I had to do this. I know she understands that I've done enough shitty shit in my life that I have to at least stand by my honor. But I'll be back for the wedding. Which means I need sleep.

I crank back my seat, staring at the ceiling, and now my mind is on what is before me, and on Asher and Adam. I'm not sorry the assholes came along for the ride. I trust Adam. I trust Asher. At one point, I didn't. At one point, I thought Asher's only asset was being the best singer on the Walker team. Which is important. Every team needs the guy who can sing happy birthday and make no one else care that everyone else can't sing worth a shit. He's also one of our top hackers, just under Blake, and he can't find a connection between Max and anyone connected to any of the addresses Max sent me. I should be comforted. Max is smart. He's staying off the radar. Asher can't find him. Asher texted with Blake and had Blake try to find him. Blake didn't find him.

All of this is good news. And yet, it's like I have a thorn in my damn side, digging a hole.

I shut my eyes and try to see Candace walking down the aisle of the church, but I can't quite get there. And I know why. Once again, something, or someone, is standing between us. I open my eyes again and stand up, walking to the back of the plane, where I sit down in a lounge area. And leave it to fucking Adam, he follows. He sits across from me.

"What are you thinking?"

"That I don't feel good about this, which is exactly why I have to go head-on into this problem."

In that moment, I know exactly what's bothering me. "I don't feel good about this," I say, "but better I walk into a trap than someone come after me and finds Candace."

Candace

I stand at the bedroom window and stare out at the New York City lights that seem to twinkle to the song on the radio—Travis Denning's *After A Few*. You can take the Texas girl out of Texas, but you can't take the country music away from the girl. Savage is a part of my soul and the truth is the country music takes me back to when we met. That coffee shop, the rain, our vehicles parked too close, and my door unable to open. We'd fought. I'd ended up in the vehicle with him and he'd kissed me. I'd fallen in love with Savage that night and hadn't even known it. For a year, he'd seduced me and become my best friend. Then he went off on a mission and never came back.

Well, not for years.

And the truth is, this is the first time he's left since we got back together.

SAVAGE ENDING

This, I tell myself, is growth for us.

I need to know he can leave on a mission and he'll always come back.

Unless he can't. And therein lies the reason I have wine in my hand. Something about this entire situation feels wrong. So very wrong.

LISA RENEE JONES

CHAPTER EIGHT

Savage

Like clowns in a mini car, me, Adam, and Asher pile into the large sedan I rented, a sedan that isn't large at all. "I will not make a joke about Asher's legs over his head right now," I say, as he tries to get comfortable in the back seat while Adam is busy removing Asher's space, by shoving the driver's seat back even further.

Asher curses as he ends up in the middle of the seat, head touching the roof. "My legs are not over my head, but my damn knees are at my ears. Who was in charge of the rental?"

I wiggle an eyebrow at him and he grunts. "Of course, you were."

I settle into my seat and move it back only to have Asher grunt again while Adam sets us in motion toward our first destination, White Castle, where burgers and fries become the rocket fuel of superhumans.

That's us.

And once we're inside the fast-food joint at a table, that's when the real magic and planning starts.

We huddle up in a small corner booth and get busy stuffing our faces. "What now?" Asher asks, finishing off one of the three burgers he ordered.

"Yeah," Adam says. "What now?"

"According to Max," I reply. "I'm supposed to text him when I land so he can give me further details. And fuck that shit is my answer to that."

"Amen, brother," Adam says. "This could all be a setup that ends with you getting your head blown off."

"Yep," I say, taking a handful of his fries since mine have been disposed of in my belly. "If Max thinks I'm a dumbass, I'll be happy to kill him."

"Not a dumbass," Asher snorts. "Just a pain in the ass."

"And proud of it, pretty-boy rocker."

Asher grins. "Pretty? You should have told me how you feel sooner, Savage. I would have told Candace to step aside." He snatches a handful of Adam's fries.

Adam scowls and not at the conversation. "I'll go get us *all* more fries." He pushes to his feet and walks toward the counter.

"Nuggets," Asher calls over his shoulder and when Adam doesn't reply, he grimaces. "He could have asked if we wanted anything. You want something?"

"I'll eat yours," I promise.

He laughs. "Which is why we all get extra, Savage." He slides out of the seat to follow Adam toward the counter.

This is how brilliant plans are created—with food and intellectual conversation.

I eat the rest of Adam's fries and my phone buzzes with a text. I glance down to read a message from Candace: *I miss you. I love you. I want to call you but I don't want to distract you. Just come home to me, sooner rather than later. I have a bad feeling about this, Rick.*

I glance toward the counter where Adam and Asher appear to have left the jest at the table behind, and traded it in for a serious conversation. They think this is a setup. I'm not sure they're wrong. And yet they're here, brothers from another mother, in this to win it no matter what the cost.

I stand up and walk to the door, stepping outside, the cool but not cold air washing over me.

I dial Candace and she answers on the first ring. "Oh God. I didn't mean for you to call. I'm the daughter of two military parents. I know distraction can get you killed."

"I'm at White Castle, baby. The only thing getting me killed right now is the food."

"You should be *here*," she says softly.

The rasp of emotion in her voice twists me in about ten knots. "I don't disagree," I assure her. "And I will be soon.

Adam and Asher are with me. We'll knock this out and be back in no time."

"Not soon enough. Not a second soon enough. Rick, I know this is what you do. I know you risk your life and you save lives. I'm not going to be like this every time you leave. This just feels different. You know why."

"I know why," I say easily. She's worried about the connection this has to my past. "After this, I'm done. I promise."

"Don't die," she whispers.

"You can't get rid of me this easily, baby. We're going to grow old together, sit on a rocker on the back porch and remember the good ol' days."

"We don't have a back porch."

"Then the balcony. And I'll tell you how my knee hurts, but how it would feel better if we were naked and in bed together."

She laughs. "I have no doubt we will have that exact conversation."

"We will and we can buy a place with a porch. We should buy a place in the Hamptons. We can escape up there, just you and me. What do you think?"

"I think I'm good with anything that we do together. Just come home to me."

"Soon," I promise. "We're in Tennessee now. We'll be on a plane to Colorado by early morning."

"Back tomorrow night?"

"Maybe. I'll try."

"Don't try so hard you get killed."

"I told you—"

"I know," she says, "I love you, Rick Savage."

"I love you, too, baby," I say. "Candace Savage."

She laughs and it's a sweet laugh. "I do love how that sounds."

"Me, too," I say. "Get some rest. I'll be home before you know it."

"Bye," she whispers, and then she hangs up.

I feel the silence on the other end of the line like a punch in the gut, sliding my phone into my pocket as I try to figure out why I felt the compulsion to do this. Why I still feel that compulsion. And then, I'm back in Mexico with Max, running a mission for the government, back when those missions were still legit.

I lean on the wall, holding it up, or maybe it's holding me up. The door opens and closes behind me and then Adam is using the wall just like me.

"We can turn back," he tosses into the night air, a twinkling little star I wish I could just grab and take home with me, but it's not that simple.

"My first mission with Max," I say, "was before we joined Tag."

"He was with you when you were military?"

"He was," I say solemnly. "Both of us worked for Candace's father. We were sent to Mexico. A cartel had kids held hostage and we were told they were prepared to slaughter them, a promise the General told us not to question. He told us to kill whoever we had to kill to save those kids. And so, we did." I glance over at him. "The reality is that day made me a willing killer. Some people deserve to die."

"Did you save the kids?"

"Every fucking last one of them and there were twenty of those little monsters. I killed as many men that day and so did Max. He also saved my life on that mission. I had two kids in my arms, and a hostile came at me. I couldn't lift my weapon. I should have died."

"And he killed him."

"He did."

"Okay," he says. "I get it. He did a good thing, but he was with Tag. He was a mercenary."

"So the fuck was I. And he wanted out of that shit, just like me."

"You're defending him with your words, but you're also standing outside, ignoring the food you worship, without a joke or snarky word to your name. Why?"

My jaw sets and my hands settle on my hips. "I don't fucking know."

"You always know," he reminds me. "You are always certain about everything you do. It's how you operated on me under heavy gunfire and saved my life."

"I don't fucking know, Adam. Maybe it's the timing. I should be with Candace, not here, right now." I hesitate, lips pressed together with another memory poking at my mind. "Or maybe I'm reliving the past, remembering the wrong moment in time."

"Meaning what?"

I turn away from him, scrubbing a hand through my hair, thinking back in time again. "Max and I had joined Tag's team, but we both thought he was an extension of the Army," I say, sitting down on the concrete wall lining a plant bed.

"A shift of funds," he supplies.

"Exactly. Same job, different title. Our first job, we saved a woman held captive by a foreign government. We'd killed that day, we killed a lot of people, but nothing there changed. We did the dirty work."

"Something changed or you wouldn't be telling me this story."

"Yeah, we got paid. That was our first payday. Max and I walked off the plane in South Carolina where we'd been stationed at that time, only to be handed envelopes loaded with cash. Max took one look inside and said, 'Fuck, man. I'll kill about anyone for this kind of cash.'"

"Fuck, Savage."

"I know. At the time, I laughed it off as talk, but there were a few moments, just a few, when I felt Max risked anything, including innocent lives, to finish his mission."

"And score his payday."

"Yeah. But there were plenty of other jobs that told a different story." I push off the wall and say, "I need to eat. Let's eat."

Adam catches my arm. "Don't blow off a gut feeling. I've seen how money can change a man."

"He saved my life," I remind him.

"Would you recommend him for Walker?"

I don't have to think. I answer immediately. "No, but you did me because you expect certain things from me. And I'm here because for the first time in years, thanks to you and Candace, I see myself as worthy of being here. I owe Max, Adam, and a debt is not always convenient. A friend in need doesn't choose when to have that need or he wouldn't be in need. I *will* pay my debt properly, the way Walker, and my woman would expect me to. And then I'm going home worthy of the woman I love. After which Candace will be in a tiny bikini on a sandy beach reminding me how fucking lucky I am to be alive and call her my wife."

He studies me a moment. "Yes, you will," he vows and releases me.

Together we head back inside and eat our damn food, brothers in all things.

I'm just not sure I can say the same of Max.

CHAPTER NINE

Savage

Candace is on my mind as Adam drives the rental toward Gatlinburg, Tennessee, while he yaks about its beauty. "I was here years back," he says, as if he hasn't told us this already. "It's a hidden gem of beauty," he continues, "a town of four thousand people, who live surrounded by green mountain tops, towering peaks, and views so glorious they draw tourists year-round."

"But does it have hotdogs on sticks and cotton candy?" I ask from the passenger seat. "Because if it does, I'll bring Candace back, take her sightseeing, and then wrap her in cotton candy, and lick it off."

Adam eyes me and says, "That sounds really messy."

"And fun," I say, eyeing the mountainous terrain beginning to take over the scenery and wishing like hell I was here with Candace and not on a mission.

Ten minutes later, the Gatlinburg city limits sign comes into view, and my gut clenches with the anticipation of what will follow, which is the unknown. I don't like the unknown.

Almost immediately, we're right in the center of a typical small-town downtown, lined with little shops and restaurants, as well as people milling about. But we don't see much of it. Adam cuts us right and heads down a country road and then another, which leads up and up some more.

Another ten minutes later, Adam parks the sedan in a cluster of trees about a mile from our pick-up destination. The three of us, armed and ready for trouble, mic up and split up, looking for an ambush. I get up close and personal with the windows of a cabin, confirming there is no one home. I take a moment to admire the hillbilly dream shack, complete with puke orange and yellow furniture, with plaid thrown in for style.

Fifteen minutes later, we're on the outskirts of the cabin, with an all-clear agreed on between us, staring at the shit-hole of a cabin that is our destination. It would be an insult to the stunning beauty of the Gatlinburg mountain terrain if it wasn't hidden away off a country road.

Asher is leaning against a tree in a squat position with his MacBook on ready and Adam and I join him before I punch in the redial for Max on speakerphone. He answers on the first ring. "Holy fuck," he says. "You really came through. You're in Tennessee."

"What am I?" I ask. "A snake-eyed liar? Of course, I'm in Tennessee. Clear my path."

"You know it, man. How far out are you?"

As planned, I play like I've just hit the runway. "I'm starving. An hour and a half. I need food before I play like your superhero."

"You really are my damn hero for this, man." There's a rasp in his voice, sincerity to the words, and yet they ring hollow. "You're headed to a small cabin in the woods," he says. "Call me when you get there. The hiding place is tricky. I need to walk you through finding it."

"I thought I was picking up from the guy who owns the cabin? Explain this to me like I'm a two-year-old. What the fuck am I doing?"

"A pick-up with no contact," he says. "The cabin is owned by the godfather of a guy I served with in the army. I visited with him years back with that buddy. He has no idea I left something behind."

In other words, if this is a legit threat, he made the enemy hunting him a long fucking time ago. And yet, I never heard about any such threat. "Where's that buddy and how does he fit into this?"

"Dead. Long dead. And don't ask a name. You don't need it. He's not a part of this."

I don't like his secrecy and I exchange a look with Adam as I ask, "Then why is he dead?"

"Iraq war."

"Then this problem is not a new problem," I say, circling back to my prior assumption.

"No," he confirms, "but it was a problem I thought long dead."

"All right," I say, aware he's not giving me details on the phone or probably ever. "How are you going to get rid of the godfather?" I ask.

"He works for the tramway there in town. If I call in a fire sighting on the cable, he'll rush to work and be tied up for hours."

It's a good answer. As good as it gets, considering how wrong this feels. "I'll call you when I get there," I say, and hang up and slide my phone back into my pocket.

"I'm dialing into the tramway," Asher informs us. "I'll know if there's a fire alert."

"He sounded legit enough," Adam says, vocalizing my own thoughts. "It matches what Asher found out about the owner. Can you find the friend, Asher?"

"We're talking godson," he says. "That could be one of hundreds, even thousands of men, but I'll try. And we have the fire alert now." He punches in a series of keys and adds, "The man who owns the cabin has a daughter and she was never in the military."

"Is the daughter married?" Adam asks. "Could the husband be the connection?"

"Divorced. I checked the ex earlier. He's a chef. No military background."

"Is the daughter here in Gatlinburg?" I ask.

"Texas," Asher says, shutting his computer. "Which is a link to you, not Max. Max is from South Carolina. I don't like this, Savage. The cabin is vacant at the moment. Call him back now. Get the data drive and let's get the fuck out of here before some shitheads show up and attack us."

"Agreed," Adam replies.

Opinions I don't make them defend or drive home. I'm on board like a motherfucker. I dial Max. He doesn't answer. I text him: *You have ten minutes to give me the drive location or I'm on a plane home.* I flash the message at

Adam and Asher. The cell rings in my hand. I answer on speaker and he says, "You're at the cabin, aren't you?"

"No," I say. "Elon Musk gave me a ride to the moon, where I'm going to sing zip-a-dee-doo-dah to the stars, man." I scowl and snap, "Where is the fucking data drive?"

"From the right side of the cabin, walk two hundred steps into the woods, then right another hundred steps. There will be a cluster of birdhouses. Right to left, count to the fourth birdhouse, and it's in a plastic bag, buried at the front of the post."

"Text me that fucking maze," I say and hang up, eyeing Adam and Asher. "Let's get this done. Cover me," and when I have their agreement, I head right, deeper into the woods, not about to stand by that cabin and count flipping footsteps. That's like saying "Here I am. Shoot me."

It's not long until I find the bird feeders, but I perch behind a thick tree trunk and just watch the clearing, waiting for something, I don't know what. Something. It feels like something is going to happen. And yet, I can't sit here like a damn bird watcher gazing at all the pretty birds, either, and there are plenty of them, all of which will scatter and make noise the minute I, or someone else, steps in their direction. And as much as I'd like to wait this out and see who shows up to kill me, and kill them first, my future wife might not like that idea.

Time is critical.

Now that Max knows we're here, so could someone else. Even him. For all I know, Max is here, waiting on me. And Max is a damn good killer. Not as good as me, but good enough to ruin my damn wedding.

CHAPTER TEN

Candace

I'm already in my pajama pants and a tank top with a TV dinner and wine in front of me on the kitchen island when the doorbell rings.

Since we're in a high-security building, that means my guest is someone on my approved list. That means it's someone from Walker Security and suddenly my heart is in my chest. If something happened to Savage, someone would come here and tell me. I run for the door, literally run, my heart in my throat as I force myself to pause and call out, "Who is it?"

"Julie, and nothing is wrong besides you being alone."

Relief washes over me and I open the door to find her standing there, looking as gorgeous as always with a bit more pink in her cheeks than usual. "You're sure he's okay?"

"No," she says. "I have no idea where Savage is, so I can't say I'm sure. But what I am sure of is my craving for pizza and ice cream. Go get dressed. Feed me and pray for me. If I'm not pregnant, the test lied and I'm just getting fat."

"I thought we already knew this was the real deal."

"That's what the line on that little stick declared. What if the stick lied?"

"You're being paranoid."

"Probably. I'm just afraid the bubble will burst."

"It won't. Have you told Luke? What did he say?"

"He's working tonight with some new client Walker took on. I'll tell him soon, probably at Sunday brunch in bed." She waves me onward. "Hurry. Dress yourself, woman. I'm not

47

taking you out like that and Lord help us all, some people would."

I glance at my watch. "It's late. You know that, right?"

"It's nine o'clock in New York City. It's practically lunchtime. And when they're off saving lives, we have each other."

She's right. New York City never sleeps. And since I'm not likely to either until Savage is home, I allow myself to be convinced to get out of the house. I hurry upstairs, toss on jeans, a lacy burgundy top, and boots. A hint of makeup and a brush through my hair completes the look. A few minutes later, Julie and I are headed down the elevator. Thirty minutes later, we're sitting at a pizza joint we both love, one that just happens to have an ice cream parlor next door.

Once the pizza is piping hot and on our table, Julie and I dig in, but one slice in, she pauses and studies me. "Savage leaving is hard, right?"

"God, yes," I say, setting down my soda. "Brutal. And I don't want you to think I'm going to be difficult every time he goes on a job, but right now it's more about the timing, I think."

"Of course it is," she says. "And Savage has made a crapload of money doing high-risk jobs. He already asked to stay local as much as he can and take the less risky jobs."

I blink and straighten. I knew he'd planned this but not that he'd made it official. "He did?"

"Oh, damn it." She cringes. "Maybe I wasn't supposed to tell you. Maybe that was a surprise."

Tension uncurls in my shoulders. "A good one, too, considering I spent most of my adult life fearing he was dead. And well-timed. I'm glad you told me. It helps."

She loads another slice of pizza on my plate and another on her own and despite feeling quite a bit better right now, I can't help but ask, "Has Luke, or the other brothers, heard from Savage?"

"Blake was actually at our house when Asher called him. He had him try and track down a property owner. That's all I know."

My brows dip. "That sounds like trouble."

"That sounds like Savage's team ensuring there are no surprises. Relax. He's got good friends, skilled friends, with him. They'll make sure he's at the church, looking pretty in a tuxedo."

"God, he does look pretty in a tuxedo," I say with a sigh. She grins and then starts talking babies. For the rest of the meal, I relax into the night, thankful Julie talked me into this. I'm getting married. She's starting a family. We are both at a place in life we can call a new beginning.

Once we're next door, we both order two huge scoops of Oreo ice cream in cups and head outside to a heated patio to eat. Julie takes one bite and sets her cup down. "I think I need to go to the bathroom."

"You okay?"

"The price of making babies," she says. "Eat. I'll be right back." She stands up and rushes away.

I hesitate, feeling as if I should follow her, but she's left her purse behind. Reluctantly, I grab my spoon, and that's when a strange sensation of being watched overtakes me, little prickles teasing the back of my neck.

My gaze scans the few people around us, all in deep conversation and ignoring me. I further my search with a glance around the immediate area beyond the ice cream parlor. Still, I see nothing, but that sensation hasn't gone away. Furthering my reach, I glance across the street and find a figure in the shadows. Just standing there, looking in this direction, but I really can't make out much about the person.

Uncomfortable, I slide both purses over my shoulder and pick up the two ice creams. Once I'm inside, where seating is limited, I head toward barstools and a bar in the rear, near the restrooms. I've just set everything down again when Julie exits the bathroom. "Did you get cold?"

"More like spooked. There's some creep standing across the street staring at me. And how are you?"

"I'm fine now," she says, "but I don't like how that sounds. I'll call one of the guys to walk us home." She's already dialing her phone and I appreciate how much she respects my concerns.

My mind flashes back to a moment when Savage and I had just arrived in New York City. We'd been cooking breakfast in what had become our kitchen but he'd suddenly gotten serious on me, turning me to face him, hands on my shoulders.

"I made a lot of enemies," he says. "You know that, right?"

"After all we just went through, you know I know."

"We're going to spend a lot of time at the firing range. And I want you to take karate. And if you ever get a gut feeling that something is wrong, do not ignore it. Understand?"

I laugh. "You're being too intense. I get it. I'll be careful."

"Candy, baby—"

"I will not ignore a gut feeling, I value my ability to handle a gun, and will happily learn to fight and kick your ass."

He kisses me and I end up naked on the counter, but that's another part of that story.

"Done," Julie says, snapping me back to the present. "Luke was actually done with his work and he's coming to walk us home."

And he does. Forty-five minutes later, we've eaten ice cream and even stayed around for Luke to have some for himself. And he and Julie have dropped me at my apartment. Luke even does a little walk-through for me to be sure all is well.

When I'm alone, I lean on the door and stare at the apartment that feels so damn empty right now. I squeeze my eyes shut and I'm back at that ice cream parlor, staring at the man across the street. Or I think he was a man.

I consider calling Savage, but if he's in danger, distraction will only muddle his mind, and perhaps his position. Luke knows what's going on. If this is a problem, he'll tell Savage and he'll tell him at the right time.

Besides, perhaps that encounter wasn't an encounter at all. Maybe that man was just waiting on someone. Or waiting on a cab, or a movie, or a reservation. I don't know, but I think I'll stay close to home until Savage returns.

CHAPTER ELEVEN

Savage

I'm still standing under the cover of the woods, staring out at the birdhouses clustered in trees and sitting on stilts dug into the ground, when Adam eases to my side and murmurs, "You feel it, too."

I nod without looking at him, aware that he's talking about that *something* I'm waiting on. Seconds turn into a minute before I whisper, "In an ideal world I'd wait for nightfall."

He gives a soft snort. "When do we ever operate in an ideal world?"

He's right. We need to move now. Since I have yet to receive the instructions from Max, I motion to the tree, which I assume to be my destination. Adam motions to himself and it and starts to move. I grab his arm and not gently. "You're not going."

"Think about Candace," he snaps in a low, tight voice.

Exactly why he shouldn't be here. Nothing like a couple of dead friends as a wedding gift to my wife. I release him and take off running. I'm halfway across the clearing when my gaze catches on a glint at the other side of the clearing. I duck behind a tree as stupid-ass Adam flies by me. He can't just stay the fuck back. Hooked to my mic, I say, "Where are you, Asher?"

"East side of the circle, and yes I saw it, too. I'm going in behind that position."

"Before the asshole shoots Adam," I say, and I ease around the tree to find Adam squatting beside the targeted birdhouse, already digging. And God help us all, everything in my gut says he's in trouble. I take off running toward the center of the circle, ensuring I'm the target. A gun discharges, but the bullets pelt a tree to my left. I dive behind yet another tree. Thank fuck, Adam does the same. Gunfire unloads for a full minute and then stops.

Asher speaks in our connected mics. "Four hostiles down. One on the move. I can't see him. Assume he can see you."

"Disco inferno, baby," I say, and because Adam knows me, he knows exactly what I mean. We'll take center stage, back-to-back, and just start firing, lighting up everything and everyone in our range.

"Are you fucking nuts?" Adam demands, rejecting that idea. "That's a desperate solution. We have Asher."

And a hostile in hiding who could kill either of them any second, I think, but I don't waste words or time. If he's not in, I'm on my own. Weapon in hand, I take off running.

Adam and Asher immediately unload their weapons, giving me cover, or I hope like fuck it's Adam and Asher. Bullets pelt near my feet and I dive right and roll down a hill, into the woods.

I'm on my feet in a blink, and I'm following the sound of gunfire on this side of the woods. I don't bother to hide or play coy. Coy is for pussies. I'm here to kill the bad guys and go home to Candace.

I round a corner and a dude in fatigues is suddenly a cornered deer in headlights, turning himself and his gun on me. Before he can threaten me more than he already has, I shoot him between the eyes. Just that easily, he's dead. The end. Footsteps sound behind me and I draw my second weapon and whirl around to find two more hostiles charging in my direction. In other words, they think they need me alive, probably to get that data drive. I, on the other hand, do not need them alive. I shoot them both dead.

Adam and Asher appear to my left and right. "We're clear," Adam announces. "Dumbass. You could have gotten yourself killed."

"Agreed," Asher says, as he kneels beside a body and rips off the mask, exposing his face. "Any idea who he is?"

I glance at the thirty-something man with red hair and I've already dismissed him. "Never seen him in my life." I turn to Adam, who's removed the masked of the two other hostiles. I glance at the unfamiliar faces, dismiss them as well, and then eye Adam. "Did you get the data drive?"

He gives a negative shake of his head.

I'm already turning away, while Asher pats down the dead guy looking for ID we all know he won't find, but he has to try. In a few quick beats, I'm kneeling next to the birdhouse post where our prize should be. Adam is right there with me.

"Did you know them, Savage?"

"Nope," I say, and jackpot. I have the baggie with the drive. I'm also not oblivious to the fact that I drank my way through many a mission Tag gave me, and then buried secrets about the missions I did for Tag just to protect myself. And many of those missions were done with Max by my side. He says he buried this secret before he ever knew me and yet he somehow did exactly what I used to do, before he knew I did it?

It doesn't add up.

Uneasy as fuck now, I stand, ready to get the fuck out of here.

Adam follows me to my feet. "I saw two come at you. Why did they seem like they knew you?"

Good question, I think, but what I say is, "I am pretty remarkable. You know it. I know it."

"Savage—"

"They thought I was surrounded and holding the prize." I indicate the bag. "And now I am."

"It was more than that," he states. "You know. I know it."

I hate when he uses my words as his words. Damn copycat. I turn and start walking, unwilling to get into Adam's paranoid head.

He falls into step with me, but thank fuck, Mr. Chatty Cathy leaves his loose lips behind. Sometimes he rambles on in such a high and mighty way, I want to knock him out and dress him up in a tutu and crown. Then we'll see who's high and mighty.

Our next stop is the rental car, where we load up inside, the two of us, and sit there, saying nothing for a full minute until Asher slides into the backseat. I don't ask where he's been. He fingerprinted the dead guys, and I couldn't give two flips who died here today. I'm delivering the data drive, some cash to Max. and then I'm done with all this bullshit.

And yet—"Damn it," I curse because I know what I have to do. I hand the baggie to Asher. "Can you copy it?" I ask.

"Of course, I can copy it," he says, already opening the baggie. And he doesn't ask why I want what I want.

We all know why. It's insurance. In case when this is over, it isn't really over.

"You want to know what's on it?" Asher asks.

"No, I don't fucking want to know what's on it. And neither do you. Insurance is just that. Insurance. What we don't know can't hurt us."

I turn away from him and settle into my seat, as Adam says, "Unless it can."

I scowl at him and say, "Drive," in the snarliest voice I can muster.

He doesn't seem to notice.

CHAPTER TWELVE

Savage

Seems we killed the bad guys, as in *all of them.*

No one follows us out of town.

"What the fuck was that, Savage?" Adam demands as we pull out of the town and hit the highway.

"Me saving your Navy SEAL Team Six ass. I thought you were supposed to be smart to be Team Six? Damn near royalty? They were shooting at us and you ran right by me."

"Because you're getting married in a few days, and I'm not taking your dead body to your future wife."

"And it's better if I take yours to her?"

"Yes, you hardheaded bastard. Yes, it is. And I'm not dead."

"Because I saved your ass."

Asher clears his throat. "Okay, ladies. Are you sure you two aren't getting married?"

"Don't go renegade again," Adam snaps.

"Yes, mother," I say. "And would you like me to bring in the garbage, too?"

"Speaking of garbage," Asher interjects, clearly trying to find some level of calm between us. "As expected, no IDs on any of these guys, but I did run the prints. We'll have them as insurance right along with the data drive. As for what's on the drive—"

"You looked," I say. "Damn it, Asher—"

"It's the coordinates to five locations," he says. "I have no idea what they are and all appear to be in the middle of nowhere. Two are outside the United States."

My lips press together. "Which locations?"

"Texas, Arizona, Florida, Mexico, and Iraq," he says.
I draw in a breath and settle forward in my seat, staring
at the dark road, unhappy as fuck.

"What just happened, Savage?" Adam demands, "And
don't tell me nothing."

"Any idea that this problem originates from before my
time is bullshit," I say. "I did jobs for Tag in every one of
those places. I kept proof of every job. I buried that proof.
Not where Max thinks I buried it but I buried it."

"Alrighty then," Asher says. "This is one of those times
I'm damn glad we scrambled the GPS on our phones. You
know Max had your number labeled. If someone has his
phone, someone will figure out you're involved."

"Max isn't that stupid," I assure him. "He wouldn't label
my number with my name."

"You hope," Adam says, and then adds, "You also drank
your way through half your years with Tag and Max. We
already know you forgot half the shit that happened. Did
Max keep track of where you buried your insurance? Is he
using that against someone, bribing them?"

"Fuck if I know," I say. "I'm not that fucktard's keeper. I
also wasn't as drunk as he thought. I buried insurance. Just
not where he thought. And I've never seen Gatlinburg, so
that data drive wasn't buried by me."

"Are you sure about that?" Adam challenges. "You forgot
things from back then, Savage."

I scowl. "I didn't blackout. Things just got a little hazy
here and there, but never when I actually worked a job. Does
he think he's using my insurance to blackmail someone?
Based on that map Asher is looking at, that feels a little too
right to be wrong. But for all I know he buried his own
insurance."

"Even if he only thinks he has your insurance," Asher
counters, "you're attached to this. You're in this."

"I'm not fucking in this," I snap. "Not after I deliver that
data drive and then beat Max's ass."

"And if he hands over coordinates to nothing to
someone?" Asher challenges. "Then what?"

"Then fuck him and his dumb ass. We deliver the data drive. We go to Colorado. I keep my word and pay back the man who saved my life, not once but thrice. Then we go home."

I dial Max.

He doesn't answer.

Already Asher is pushing again. "Why didn't he do a secure internet drop to his buyer?"

"He's not tech-savvy enough to do it securely," I reply. "And he's not operating with a team."

"I'll do it for him," Asher replies. "Then we don't have the drop-off exposure."

"Oh sure," I say dryly. "I'll tell him he can trust you. I'm sure he'll agree. Bottom line. I owe him a favor. It's not my fault if he uses it in a stupid way. Onwards we go."

And so, we do, for a few long hours on the highway, all of which Max isn't answering my calls.

A big ass problem since I have an address for the drop-off and nothing more. At two in the morning, Adam parks us a few blocks from the warehouse destination, in a sea of warehouses.

"What do you want to do?" he asks. "You have no instructions."

"What I've always done," I say. "Bury the prize in a place he'll only find if I want him to find it." I open the door and Adam and Asher follow.

The three of us coordinate a scouting mission and it's not long before we're in the woods behind the dark warehouse. I pick a tree, dig a hole, and bury the data drive. Then I carve an X in the tree. That's it. As far as I'm concerned, we're done.

Fifteen minutes later, the three of us load up in the car, and I dial Max. When he doesn't answer, I don't leave a message. I have no idea who might have his phone. "Let's get the fuck out of here."

"I talked to Blake," Asher says. "He wants us out of here. We have a plane waiting for us about thirty minutes away."

I don't argue. Only a stupid fucktard would stay around to get killed. And I take great pride in never being a stupid fucktard. I want us out of here, too.

By the time me, Adam, and Asher pull up to the private airstrip for our flight from Nashville to Colorado, I've decided that yes, I could have walked away from this. But my gut told me not to for a reason. As much as I've tried to deny, the locations listed on that map say I'm a part of this, even if it's indirectly. And any unknown could be dangerous, and it's not me I'm worried about.

It's Candace.

I exit the vehicle and corner Asher. "If there's a connection to me, I need to know."

"I'm working on it. So is Blake."

I give a nod and say, "Thanks, man."

A few minutes later we all load up on the private jet and do what we've been trained to do to be battle-ready. Grab sleep where we can get it. We snooze and eat on the three-hour flight. The plane lands in Denver, where we're an hour and a half from Estes Park.

Blake, ever the efficient one, and a perfectionist, has a car waiting on us. Once we're on the road, we hit a truck stop, shower, change, and grab food at the diner attached to the joint. We don't do any magical planning this time. The food goes down. And then we're on the highway, tracking our path forward.

It's then that I dial Candace. She picks up on the first ring. "Tell me you're coming home."

"Almost, baby," I say. "Tomorrow," I add, hoping like hell I can turn that into tonight. "But I'm in Colorado. We're going to drop some cash to Max, and be out of here."

"So there's been no problem?"

"I'll tell you all about it when we get home."

"Oh God," she whispers. "What happened?"

"Candy, baby—"

"You're not going to tell me," she says flatly.

"Not right now," I confirm. "Later."

"All right," she concedes. "You're alive. That's what matters. I love you, Rick Savage. Come home to me. I waited a long time to marry you."

"I love you, too. I'll call you again if I can. Okay?"

"Yes, okay." She hesitates and then says, "See you soon." And then she hangs up.

Adam grins in my direction. "Never thought I'd see the day you'd be the married guy calling wifey with words of love."

I eye him. "You're next."

"Not him," Asher jokes. "*Never* Adam. He's immune to ways of the heart. He said so."

My mind flashes back to the night I met Candace, reliving a night that changed me forever.

It's raining fucking cats and dogs, which is no finish for a hellish night at the hospital, and one emergency after another. Sleep would be a luxury when I have the ten stacks of paperwork to do that my father handed over to me. That's what happens when your father is an acclaimed surgeon and you're just an intern: you get the grunt work. And you drink a lot of coffee.

I whip into the parking lot Halcyon for coffee and whatever bakery item hits my fancy, and the stop is near the door, vacant because some asshole parked over the lines. Well, I'm the asshole that will teach the other asshole a lesson. The rain blessing me pulls back, retreating into the dark sky. I pull my hoodie up anyway, open my door, and step outside.

I'm greeted by a fireball of a pretty woman, her long, dark hair in beautiful disarray, her green eyes blazing.

"What are you doing?" she demands.

Amused by this intrusion, the tiredness seeps from my bones, and I'm fully engaged. "Staring at a pretty lady, it seems," I say, my tone reflecting my immediate interest.

Her eyes flash with a hint of surprise at the compliment, her temper momentarily cooled, only to fire right back up again. "I can't get into my car. You parked on top of me."

"You parked over the line and I didn't want to get my pretty little head all wet."

"I didn't park over the line."

"You did," I assure her. *"Go look."* I motion toward her car. *"I'll wait here."*

"I'm not going to look. You have to move. I can't open my door."

I cross my arms in front of my chest, and at six-foot-five, I peer down at her with my most intense look, my tone serious as fuck, just as I intend. *"What are you going to give me if I do?"*

"How about I save your manhood from my knee?"

I laugh, low and deep, a laugh I needed for reasons most wouldn't understand. And crazy as fuck as it might sound, I want to kiss this stranger. I want to kiss her in a bad way. *"How about,"* I say, my gaze lowering to her mouth, and lingering before it lifts, as I add, *"you have coffee,"* I pause for effect, *"with me."*

There's more of that surprise in her eyes but it's replaced with indignation. *"Are you seriously bribing me for entry into my own vehicle?"*

Thunder roars above us and the rain begins to plummet down again. I don't even think about what comes next. I catch her hand and pull her close, all her soft curves pressed to my hard body, really fucking hard right about now. I lift her, turn her, and sit her inside my truck where she's warm and dry and then quickly follow. She scurries to the other side of the vehicle, where she cannot escape because, of course, I'm parked right on top of her vehicle. I don't want her to escape, either. But I also don't want her to want to escape. I want her to stay, right here, with me, and I want her to do it because she wants to do it.

"What are you doing?" she demands indignantly, and I can almost feel her heart racing in her chest. Fuck me, mine is too.

"You can't grab me and throw me in your vehicle," she exclaims.

I turn to face her, and damn she's prettier every moment I look at her. And she smells good, like the flowers

*at the side of my parents' house my mother frets over. "I
was saving you, woman. It's a mad downpour out there.
But if you want me to let you out, I will."*

*Thunder crashes again and she jumps, eyes squeezing
shut a moment, then lifting to study me studying her.
"Well?" I challenge softly, willing her to stay.*

"You're still an asshole."

*She's adorable and as she stares at me, I feel the heat
between us. She doesn't want to go. And I damn sure don't
want her to go. My lips quirk. "Does that mean the fair
maiden wishes to remain in the shelter of my fine vehicle?"*

"I should be afraid of you right now."

I arch a brow. "Are you?"

*She blinks, seemingly as distracted and confused right
now as I am. I am not a man who gets obsessed with a
woman, at all, let alone in five flat seconds. "Am I what?"
she asks.*

"Afraid of me," I supply.

"I should be," she repeats.

*"Why are you out at this time of night alone?" I ask,
curious about her, and also eager to make sure she isn't
meeting a man. Not that I'd back off. I wouldn't.*

"Why are you?" she snaps back.

*"Why not? Who do you think a bad guy would attack?
You or me?"*

"Depends on which one of us has the biggest gun."

*I laugh again, more intrigued by this woman by the
second. "Do you carry?"*

"Yes. And I know how to use it," she adds.

*"You're a fierce one," I comment, amused, aroused,
distracted by a stranger, and it's a welcome distraction I
might not be able to afford, but I just don't care.*

"You're an arrogant one," she rebuts.

*"I'm not arrogant," I assure her, unable to keep some
of the dark energy that description stirs in me from my
voice. My father is arrogant. My father who I both idolize
and hate, true hate, the kind no man should feel for his
father. "A smart-ass, yes. Arrogant, no."*

61

"Parking too close to me wasn't you being arrogant? Just a smart-ass?"

My mood lightens instantly and I grin. "Yep. How'd I do?"

"Perfectly."

"Glad to hear it," I say. "I'm Rick Savage, by the way, but most people call me Savage."

"They call you Savage? Are you supposed to be making me feel better?"

"Savage can have many meanings, sweetheart," I assure her, a wicked suggestion in my tone and eyes when I look at her. Her cheeks heat, a blushing, shy beauty that I do not expect, after her confronting me, but I damn sure love the contrast of character.

"Shy, are you?" I tease.

"I'm—not, actually. Not really."

"You did come at me like a freight train, I'll give you that. Call me Rick." I offer her my hand, aware that if I touch her again, I'll kiss her. Her eyes flicker with apprehension, nervous energy, but there is more in their depths; there is that mutual attraction. Tentatively she reaches forward and presses her soft palm to mine, our grips light. But light or not, even this small touch is ridiculously arousing.

"Candace Marks," she says softly, and when she tries to pull back, I close my hand around hers, I hold on, but gently enough that she knows she can pull away.

"Nice to meet you, Candace," I say, my eyes warm on her face.

"I'm not sure if it's nice to meet you or not yet, Rick."

My lips curve, and I am thinking about her pretty little mouth painted mauve, and how much I want it on mine. But she tugs her hand, and damn it, I have to let her go. Reluctantly, so damn reluctantly, I release her. There's regret in her expression, as if she didn't want me to let her go, and fuck. I want to pull her back to me. But she turns away, facing the window as hail pucks down against the glass. And suddenly, or not so suddenly at all, I want to know more about her, and not just how she tastes. "What brings you here so late and in a storm?" I ask.

She shifts to face me again, a bit more relaxed now as if conversation eases the awkwardness of a kiss we didn't share. "School and work," she says.

"What are you studying and/or working on?"

"Architecture. I'm interning right now under a rather famous architect. It's a bit intimidating but exciting."

She's smart. Creative. Owns a gun and smells good while looking pretty. I'm all in. I'm never all in with a woman, but for some reason, with Candace, right here and now, I am. "Interesting choice of career. What do you want to build?"

"Everything. I have so many dreams. The tallest building in the world that reaches well into the clouds. The most unique building in the world. The most secure building in the world. The most impressive homes on planet Earth."

"That's what I call passion," I say, and I recognize that passion because it's what I feel for medicine. "Are you following in someone's footsteps?"

"No. I think it started with a fascination with the pyramids and morphed into architecture. What about you? Why are you here late at night?"

"Med school. I'm a surgical resident at Fort Sam where my father's an instructor."

"Impressive. It is, after all, considered the most important military medical training facility in the world. My father's at Fort Sam, too, but he's not part of the medical division. He's the commander for the North. Are you military?"

"I am, in fact, military."

"Our fathers might know each other."

He gives a nod. "I'm certain they must."

"I thought soldiers were pack animals and yet you're here, alone. It's dangerous out alone, you know," she teases.

I don't laugh. She's hit a nerve and I cut my stare, gripping the steering wheel, my forearm flexing with the *tightness of my grip. Normally alone is exactly where I want to be and that's exactly what I wanted tonight. Until I didn't.* "Sometimes alone isn't the best place to be," I say and I look at her, without even trying to hide everything I went through tonight. The little girl who died despite how fucking hard I worked to save her. My father, who didn't act fast enough, in my book, because he was in his office drinking. "Now is it?" I ask.

"No," she says. "No, it's not." She hesitates and adds, "Especially not tonight."

It's a confession I believe I've inspired by being honest. And I want to know more.

"Why not tonight?" I ask.

"You don't know me. You don't need to pretend to care."

"I don't pretend. Ever. And as for barely knowing each other, we are the freest we will ever be together. You don't have to choose to see me again. You don't have to think about the mistakes we've made together. You don't have to do anything, including answering my question." And yet I ask again, "Why not tonight?"

She exhales a shaky breath, her fingers twisting in my lap, her gaze shifting forward to the window drizzled with rain. The storm has slowed now, at least the one unleashed by the sky, but I have this sense that there is one inside her, as there is one inside me, and neither are even close to calm.

"My mom died last month," she says. "My dad is deploying to Iraq next week." She glances over at me, pain in those beautiful green eyes. "If that's not enough, I live in a house I inherited from my dead grandmother who I loved very much."

I want to scoop her up. I want to kiss her. Hell, I want to get her naked and make her and me forget all the shit going on in our lives. I want to be lost in Candace. But before I choose what comes next, I need to know one thing. "Do you have a boyfriend, Candace?"

"No. I mean, I did, but it wasn't serious. He was military and a little too busy trying to impress my father for me to feel like anything was about me. What about you?"

"No one," I say with no hesitation.

No one.

The words linger in the air and I'm aware of the heaviness they hold. She studies me with interest, and I'm aware, even before she asks the question, that she wants to pluck them from the air, hold them, and understand them. "Why are you here alone, Rick Savage?"

I fix her in a deep stare, and I say exactly what I feel. "To meet you," I say softly with a rough, affected quality to my voice I barely understand. But I don't fight it. "I just didn't know it yet."

The storm erupts again, an explosion of rain, wind, and hail a curtain over the windows, a crack of thunder following. Intense. We don't speak, but there is a pulse between us, and I say fuck it. I need to kiss her. I move toward her, and instead of backing away, she moves into me. We're in the middle of the seat when my fingers tangle into the soft strands of her hair and my mouth lowers to hers. "I'm going to kiss you now, unless you object," I say "because I have an absolute need for this to be what you want, too."

"Kiss me already, Savage," she whispers.

"Rick," I say. "Call me Rick." And then my mouth collides with her mouth, licking into her mouth, the taste of her sweet honey on my tongue.

She lets out a tiny moan and then her arms slide around my back, her soft, curvy body pressing against my body, and it's all I can do to keep my hands in her hair. And I have no idea why that feels so important with Candace, but it does. At least at this very moment. I pull back and she stares down at me. "Do you want to get out of here? Together?"

Her fingers curl on my T-shirt but she doesn't move away. In fact, she seems to melt into me. "I don't do things like this," she whispers. "Ever."

I like that answer, I think. I like that I'm the one that made her kiss a stranger in the middle of a storm. I kiss her again and when she's breathless, I say. "Then make me the first."

I blink back to the present, my eyes on the road ahead of me, but my mind is still with Candace. I was never immune to her or her to me, and I don't regret falling for her, or her for me. I regret following her father to my first kill. Because I can never know she's safe. Ever. I will always have an enemy. And she will always share those enemies.

CHAPTER THIRTEEN

Savage

Estes Park is a small little mountain town with a population of six thousand, give or take a few hundred. The path to get there is a climb through the mountain, by way of narrow winding roads with no railings and steep drops. The higher we get, the thinner the air, sure to slow down the enemy. Just not us. We're bad-asses.

"I was here once, a year ago," Asher informs us. "I stayed at the Stanley Hotel. It's supposed to be haunted as fuck."

"And?" Adam prods. "Because I know there's more."

"Oh hell yeah there's more," Asher confirms. "I was in bed and felt like I was being watched. I lifted my head and there was a cowboy standing at the end of my bed. No lie. I swear to God."

"Hell to the no on that," I say, downing a sip of Dr. Pepper. "I like enemies that can die and then I make them dead."

Adam eyes Asher in the rearview. "What did you do?"

"The only thing I could do," Asher replies. "I went back to sleep."

If only I could go the fuck back to sleep and this Max thing had never happened. "Anything I need to know about?" I ask, glancing at Asher who now, as always it seems, has his MacBook opened.

"If you're asking if I've connected Max or anything of this to you, no. Neither has Blake. There's no chatter on the web, not even the dark web, about you."

"And Max?" I ask.

"No," he says.

"In other words, no chatter about me means nothing."
My mind goes back to yet another moment with Max.

I shift in my damn seat, cramped as hell, and at this point, we're high as fuck. We have to be close to Max's place. "How much further?"

"Five miles," Asher says. "And between here and there we need a place to hide the rental that isn't off the side of a cliff."

"Not to be a Negative Nelly," I say, "but I'm back to hell to the no on that. We're driving up to the door."

"And hell to the no on that shit," Asher snaps. "He won't return your calls. He's dirty or dead. We're not going to walk up to the door."

"He likes booby traps," I say. "And he's good at them. Unless you want a fishhook in your eye, captain, we go in straight and to the door."

Adam gives me a side-eye, grimaces, and keeps driving.

Ten minutes later, we turn down a narrow road, drop-offs on either side of us. "If you come at him from this road, you want him dead," I murmur.

"Let's not get dead with him," Adam says, and that's all he has to say. When he halts the car, we all prepare, locking and loading, ready for action. Sixty seconds later, I'm feeling all warm and fuzzy about this reunion with Max with a gun in each hand, as we keep on rolling, straight to yet another hillbilly delight cabin. We park right in front. A perfect location to see an immediate problem.

The cabin door is open.

"That doesn't look good," Adam murmurs.

"Now who's a Negative Nelly?" I reply. "Maybe he has cameras and he saw us coming, and wanted to invite us in." I open my door, stand up, and I remain bullet-free as I expect. An enemy wouldn't be this obvious. Either Max is inviting us in or he's dead.

Adam and Asher are on my heels as I head up the steps and ease inside the cabin, to find furniture overturned, a window broken, and no signs of life. I hold a hand up to the others to stay in their positions and call out, "Max!"

Silence greets me, complete silence. I pull my weapons, one in each hand, and ease into the living area, forced to step over the top of a puddle of what looks like coffee, with a broken cup in the center. Somehow Max got surprised, which took effort by the bad guy. Max doesn't get surprised. Someone wanted him dead in a bad way and had the skill to catch him. Or come close.

The kitchen is part of the living room and I walk down a small hall to a bathroom, which is tiny and without human occupancy. Next stop is a bedroom which is a box, easy to search with a scan, but for good measure, I check under the bed and in the closet. When all is clear, I shove one Glock in my boot and the other in my waistband before I rejoin Adam and Asher in the main room. "He's not here," I announce. "I'm going to search the bedroom."

I disappear back into the hallway and then the bedroom, where I lift the mattress, check under the sheets, furniture, and inside drawers. There's nothing here, and I mean nothing. No clothes. No papers. Nothing. There's also no dust, which means someone, Max, I assume, was living here long enough to clean up.

My next stop is the bathroom, and a quick search delivers nothing. Back in the living room, Asher and Adam are just finishing up. "Nothing," Adam says.

"Same here," Asher agrees, both of them now staring at me. "Except the lack of dust. This place hasn't been empty. Anything in the back?"

"Not even a pair of socks," I say, "and believe me, his ugly-ass feet need socks."

"Then he packed before he left," Adam comments, hands settling on his hips. "You don't grab your underwear and socks as you run for your life."

"What about the signs of a struggle?" Asher says, kicking a piece of the broken mug. "He could have had a bag ready to go when an unwanted visitor showed up."

"Whatever the case," I say. "We're done here. Let's go home."

Adam frowns. "That's it?" Adam challenges. "We're done here? There was an obvious struggle."

"No blood," I say. "No body. Max knows this land. I told you. He's booby-trapped this terrorist. He would have led his enemies to their death. And I did what I promised I'd do."

"Except no one knows where you put that data drive," Asher reminds me.

"If Max is alive," I say, "he'll call. If he's dead, it's a non-issue."

"And if that data drive has something to do with you?" Adam asks.

"If it did, whoever is after him would have come for me," I say. "This is over."

"What if it's not?" Adam argues. "He pulled you into this. Maybe he used you as some sort of fall guy."

I have no reason to believe Max would betray me or I wouldn't be here, except that one moment when we were handed those envelopes. *"I'd kill about anyone for this kind of money."* It sits worse every time I have the memory. And, I remind myself, there were other moments when I questioned him, but couldn't put my finger on why.

But he also saved my life.

Three times.

I glance between Asher and Adam. Every minute they're here, they become more a part of my past. They don't belong in my past and neither do I. That's what doesn't feel right.

"We're done," I say firmly and to make my point, I cross the living room, exit the cabin, and walk to the car. It's time to go home to my future wife.

70

CHAPTER FOURTEEN

Candace

I wake alone in bed and bury myself in Savage's pillow, inhaling the scent of him. I don't know how I did this all those years Savage and I were apart. For some reason, I convinced myself he'd be home when I woke up. I force myself out of the bed, head downstairs to the gym, and workout. A girl has to look good for her wedding. After which, I shower, dress casually because I have no plans but to work, and head to the kitchen. With an egg white omelet and coffee by my side, I sit at the island and end up sketching something unplanned: a house on the beach, in the Hamptons, for me and Savage. My mind and hands go crazy and soon I have the outline of something special I can't wait to show him.

My cellphone rings, and hoping it's Savage, I grab it to find an unknown number. I'm instantly nervous that this is bad news about Savage. He'd call me Negative Nelly and he'd be right. I can't seem to help it right now. I answer quickly. "This is Candace," I say, and for some reason, I regret announcing my name. God, I'm so paranoid right now.

"Candace, this is Robin Newman from the World Museum."

"Oh hello, Robin," I say relief easing my tense shoulders. This isn't bad news. Well aside from her running the museum that canceled a big contract I had scored. Still, we'd connected, even became casual friends. My world is filled with friends these days, and it's rather lovely. And just one more way Savage has touched my life and changed it. "How are you?" I ask.

"Good." Her voice is light, cheery, even if not a tad hyped like she too is drinking gallons of caffeine. "Very good, actually," she adds. "You know that wing we wanted you to design?"

"Of course," I assure her. "You know I was excited about that job. And disappointed when funding fell through."

"Well good news!" she sing-songs. "We have a new investor."

My heart leaps. "Really? Oh my God. I want this job so much."

"And I want you to have it," she assures me, "but this investor's insistent he meet the architect and approve the plans before he writes the check. Any chance you could meet for drinks tonight?"

I'm a mix of excited and hesitant. I want Savage home. I want to see him. I want to be here when he arrives. But I don't know when that will be. And he'd be upset if I missed this opportunity. I could in fact cause the museum to lose this money if I don't go.

"Yes," I say, "but I need to remind you that I get married in less than a week and I'm going on my honeymoon."

"I remember. I was invited to the wedding."

I laugh. "Right. Bride nerves are kicking in, I think."

"Of course they are. How can they not be? It's a fun, exciting time. And the time off won't be a problem. We just need to lock down the money."

We organize the time and location, and I return to my home drawing. I don't actually do residential architecture, but doing ours would be special. We need a porch to reenact Savage's story, I think, smiling. The doorbell rings, and I stand and head in that direction. When I open the door, I expect Julie. Instead, I find Blake, with what looks like a two-day stubble shadowing his jaw, and bloodshot eyes.

My heart falls and I can't breathe. "Tell me he's okay."

"Of course he's okay. He's not missing his wedding. This is not about Savage. It's about you. I grabbed the camera footage from your night out, and just wanted to talk to you about it. Can I come in?"

"Oh," I say surprised he came over here for this and suddenly apprehensive all over again. "Yes. Okay." I back up to allow him to enter. "You want coffee?"

"Hell yes," he says. "I'd kill for coffee. I've been up all night working on a project for a new client."

"And you came here without sleep?" I ask, walking to the pot with a frown on my face. That apprehension just notched up a level. "This must be a serious visit."

"We take the safety of our team and their families seriously. So yes, it's serious."

Having been around Blake quite often, I know how he takes his coffee, so I fix it up and set it in front of him, leaning on the island to his right. "Am I in danger?"

"I'm actually here to put your mind at ease." He scrubs a hand through his dark hair. "I guess I should have said that out of the gate. No sleep. I suck. Sorry, Candace. All is well. I found a street camera that captured the man who was across the street from you last night."

"And?"

He grabs his phone and pulls up a video. "I lightened it up, so you can see it well." He punches the play button.

I watch as an old man smokes a cigarette and then quickly puts it out when a couple of kids run up to him and hug him.

"His grandkids," Blake informs me. "He's lived in the apartment behind where he's standing for years. He goes outside to smoke so his wife won't know."

I let out a breath and laugh. "Now I feel silly."

"Don't. You had a bad feeling. Sometimes those bad feelings are real and for a reason, even if they don't match up to where you connect the dots. I don't want us to totally dismiss this. Stay alert. Carry your gun. Savage will be home soon and, in the meantime, if you want an escort—"

"No. No, I wouldn't take resources that could be used to save lives. I'm nervous over Savage being gone. I'm nervous over this entire Max situation. I don't trust him."

Something flickers in his eyes but disappears before I can figure out what. "Savage is safe. I know that for a fact." He sips his coffee, eyes my drawings, and says, "What's this?"

"A dream house on the island. Maybe. We'll see."

His lips curve. "Savage and a dream house on the ocean. Never thought I'd see the day." He winks. "But it's a good day." He glances at his watch. "Thanks for the coffee. It will keep me awake until I go to bed, which will be soon."

I walk Blake to the door and once he's gone, I return to the island and refill my coffee, but when I sit down, I'm unsettled. When I'd said I don't trust Max, he'd had that look in his eye and changed the topic. I should have pushed for more. And he'd told me not to ignore my gut feelings. Somehow that feels like it ties together.

My instincts, my gut, were screaming last night.

I decide right then, that while I won't ask for an escort tonight, I will make sure Blake knows where I am and when I'll be there. I text him the details. Just to be safe.

CHAPTER FIFTEEN

Candace

Savage still hasn't returned when it's time to get ready for my meeting. I'm nervous for him again, my normally steady hands a bit jittery. I can't shake this feeling he's in trouble, and I don't know how I'm going to focus tonight, yet I have to do just that. This is basically a job interview, and not just for me, but for everyone involved in the project.

With that motivation in mind, I shower and take my time with my makeup, listening to an audiobook as I do. It turns out to be a mistake, as it's a thriller that only sets me more on edge. I decide silence is a better option.

Not too much later, I'm ready early, probably because I'm high on adrenaline and those nerves. But I've at least managed to dress appropriately, I believe—I hope—in a black sweater dress and boots. My portfolio is on the kitchen island waiting for me and I sit down in front of it, planning to review my ideas I'll be presenting to the investor, just to be fresh.

Instead, I'm thinking about my conversation with Blake and his advice to stay alert. I grab my phone from the table next to me and punch in his number. "Hi, Candace," he greets lightly, and just his tone assures me Savage is fine.

"He's fine?" I ask hopefully.

"He is," he promises. "I don't know his ETA, but soon."

"Oh good," I breathe out, wishing this news would get rid of the knot in my belly, but it hasn't, which is why I confess, "I'm still feeling a bit edgy."

I can almost see his brows dip as he asks, "Did something else happen?"

"No. I've been at home, nice and safe. But what you said about staying alert feels like good words of advice. I'm going to a meeting here in a few minutes, it's for the museum project I'm bidding on. I'm being introduced to a potential investor."

"The deal you were excited about, but it fell apart?"

I blink. "How did you know that?"

"Savage brags about you more than you know."

This warms my heart. "Ah, that man needs to come home to me now."

"Like I said," he replies. "Soon. And as for tonight, I'll send you a car. How soon do you need to be there?"

"I don't want to turn Walker into my babysitter, Blake."

He swats down that idea with a stern, "Nonsense. I'll send Smith with a car."

Smith being one of the members of Walker who is frequently teamed up with Savage. A nice guy. Quiet. Dedicated. Savage likes him. "Surely he has better things to do than this," I argue.

"He's right here with me and heard the conversation. He offered. He'll be there in a flash and meet you out front."

Relief washes over me. I really didn't want to go out tonight. "Thanks, Blake."

Fifteen minutes later, I'm snuggled into my coat, waiting at the door of our building when Smith pulls a familiar Walker-owned SUV to the curb. I hurry forward, climb inside the front with him, and buckle up. "Thank you, Smith."

He waves me off. "I was off tonight and had nothing to do. I don't mind at all."

That translates to he didn't want to be alone, when I know for a fact he has women chasing him. Just not the right woman. Smith is a good-looking man with a muscular build and sandy brown hair. He's also in love with a woman that married another man.

"Well, I appreciate this so much," I say. "I'm just a tad on edge. Savage leaving and the wedding. There's just so much right now."

"I heard what happened last night," he says. "And I think you made the right decision to call Blake. I know Tag is dead, but I was a part of that war Savage had to win you back and kill that bastard. I don't like anything connected to him. And it sucks to have this happen when you two are about to get married and put the past behind you."

"God, it does," I say, "and thank you for voicing that, all of that. It makes me feel a little less paranoid."

We chat a bit more about Max and Tag, but the ride is short. Soon Smith is pulling to the door of the hotel where the bar that is my destination is located. "I'm going to park and I'll be in the bar with you," he says. "But you won't know I'm there."

"That's not necessary, Smith," I say quickly.

"A guy walks into a bar and gets a drink," he says. "That's not one of Savage's stupid punchlines. That's my real story."

My lips curve. "Okay. As long as you want that drink. I'm fine."

"See you inside," he says and winks.

I exit the vehicle and hurry through the automatic doors to enter the fancy, high-end lobby with a shiny white floor. Turning to the right, I enter the bar, where heavy carpet softens my steps and a pretty blonde hostess greets me. I'm then led through the dimly-lit bar with bright blue booths and a fancy blue and silver half-moon-shaped bar. Our destination is a table in the corner occupied by Robin and a man in a suit with neatly cut dirty blond hair. Robin pops to her feet to greet me. She's an ambitious, driven thirty-three-year-old. I'd discovered her age, not by asking, but rather being at the museum a few months back when her staff surprised her with a little party. Tonight, Robin, ever the picture of casual elegance is dressed in a navy blue dress with a cute flare at the bottom, her red hair is a silky short bob, and her freckled skin has a spray of beautiful sunshine across her nose.

"So happy you made it so last minute," she greets, grasping my hand.

"Excited to be here," I assure her, and she motions to the man who is also on his feet, awaiting his introduction. "This is Kirk Long. He's a real estate investor whose father was a renowned archeologist."

He offers me his hand and I accept it, noticing the silver ring on his index finger with a cross carved in the center. I'm not sure why I notice this at all. "Nice to meet you, Candace," he says, drawing my gaze to his green eyes. They're intelligent eyes, but I wouldn't say kind eyes. There's a hardness there that makes me wonder about his motives for this donation. Nevertheless, I return the greeting. He's staring at me now, his attention uncomfortably intense, and I'm a bit unnerved but that seems to be my perpetual state of existence these past few days.

We sit down, me next to Robin, while Kirk claims his seat across from her, as he was sitting before my arrival. For obvious reasons, this comes as a relief. I slip out of my coat as Robin grabs the waiter's attention and I order wine before Kirk lifts his whiskey glass in my direction and says, "I hear you're quite talented."

"Stunning work," Robin chimes in. "You couldn't have a better architect on this project." She laughs. "I've said that a dozen times, haven't I?"

Kirk's lips lift, his eyes crinkling at the corners slightly, enough to age him to perhaps late thirties or early forties. He's a good-looking man and yet that coldness seeps beyond his eyes and distracts from his looks. But then, I'm in love with another man. I've proven immune to other men quite completely over the years.

"I'm blessed to do what I love," I reply and pull out my portfolio, sliding it in Kirk's direction.

We begin to talk about my work and the museum design and I forget my discomfort. I am fully engaged in expressing my ideas for the new wing, which I now know will be dedicated to Kirk's father.

"These plans look worthy of my father's name," Kirk approves.

"We'll be naming the wing you're creating after his father," Robin provides, and in that answer, I find motivation. Kirk is a man who likes power and his family name on the museum wing is power. Or he just wants to honor his father, but I just don't read him that way.

I've waved off an offer of more wine when Robin receives a text message. "Oh my," she says. "The fire alarm went off at the museum. I do believe it was a prankster from what I'm being told, but I need to go ensure all is well."

"We can finish up here," Kirk offers.

My discomfort is back. Before I can hardly blink, Robin is standing, wishing us farewell and Kirk is moving to the chair in front of me. My phone buzzes with a text message now as well. I grab it and read a message from Smith: *Go to the bathroom.*

I don't need to be told twice. "I'm going to run to the ladies' room," I say to Kirk, already on my feet.

"You sure you don't want another glass of wine?" he asks.

"No thanks. Maybe coffee. I'm getting married in a few days. I'm saving my calories for the honeymoon."

His eyes flicker with something I cannot read and don't even want to try. I hurry away, around the bar and down a hallway. Smith is not present and I'm not sure what is going on. Maybe he just wants me to go into the bathroom and call in from a private location? I find the bathroom and enter to find it empty. I'm barely inside when hands come down on my waist from behind. I gasp.

CHAPTER SIXTEEN

Candace

I know instantly it's Savage.

His touch. His masculine scent. His energy.

I whirl around and he's already shut the door and pulled me against him. My hands press to his hard warm chest and his are at the back of my head.

"Miss me?" he asks.

"God, yes," I murmur.

I've barely spoken the words before his mouth is on my mouth, his tongue stroking deep, and curling my toes, but too soon he pulls back and demands, "Then why are you with another man?"

I smile, because I know he's not serious. "I know you know why I'm here and I also know you know I'm immune to anyone but you, Rick Savage."

"I do," he says. "But he doesn't."

"I told him about my wedding," I assure him.

"You did, huh?"

"Oh yes. And anyone else who will listen."

His hand splays between my shoulder blades and he molds me flush against his hard body, and for a moment, we just breathe together, feel each other, want each other. "Mine," he murmurs softly.

My hand splays on his chest, over his heart, and I echo him. "Mine."

His mouth crashes down over on mine, and any reserve we'd managed is thrown to the wind. His hands are all over me, his kiss wildly possessive. But so is mine. I too feel possessive. I lost him. I realize now when he was gone these few days just how much I feared losing him again. I twist my fingers around his T-shirt and pull him closer, if that is even possible. He drags my head back and deepens the kiss, long strokes of his tongue, driving me wild.

Everything fades into black but us and I'm only remotely aware that the skirt of my dress is at my waist. However, I'm completely aware of his hand on my backside and the thick ridge of his erection against my belly.

I'm lost in the moment right up until his fingers slide between my legs and I'm jolted back to reality. I catch his hand. "Wait. No. I have to go back out there. He's an investor for that museum project that got called off. Other people's jobs are on the line."

He draws in a breath, and his hand falls away and settles on my waist, his forehead finding mine. "Just know this. I'm waiting impatiently." He pulls back to fix me in his stare, the eyes of a man I know can be a cold-blooded killer, and still, they are warm and not just for me. "But I also know how excited you are about that museum project. Go make him want your work, not you."

I smile and run my fingers over his jaw. "Just my work. I need to fix my face and hurry back."

He catches my hand and kisses it before he eases back to allow me to move, easing my skirt back into place. I grab my purse, unzip it and step to the mirror, quickly doctoring my lipstick, and righting my wild hair. I've just zipped my purse when Savage steps behind me, hands on my waist, his eyes meeting mine in the mirror. "I can't believe you're finally going to be my wife." His voice vibrates with emotion.

It's in moments like this, when he says such things, with the intensity of a man in love, that affect me so very deeply. I wasn't alone all those years. He missed me and us, just as much as I did. Our love overcame time, other people, and even murder. I twist around and wrap my arms around him. "And you're finally going to be my husband."

"Go win the job, Candy, baby. I want you home and naked, sooner than later. I'll be with Smith at the other side of the bar."

I kiss his cheek. "I'm almost done." I move away from him but he catches my hand and when I turn to face him, he just holds onto it a moment, staring at me before he reluctantly lets it go.

I have to force myself to exit the bathroom and walk back toward the bar.

But Savage is home.

All is well in my world once again.

With my mood lighter, I slide back into the seat across from Kirk. "Sorry, that took so long. The bathroom was crowded." I barely make that statement without laughing.

Kirk studies me with keen eyes that seem to see everything, and I begin to fear I have lipstick smudged all over my face. "You seem different."

My brows dip. "Different?"

"Yes," he confirms, lifting his whiskey glass and studying me over the rim of the glass. "Less tense."

"Oh well, yes," I say. "While I was dealing with the crowded bathroom, I was thinking about my wedding."

He doesn't react, but he motions to a full glass of wine sitting beside me. "I ordered it anyway, just in case."

The man is determined for me to drink, and while I would have refused if I was alone, I'm not alone anymore. Savage is here. I feel him even if I can't see him. There are two large pillars dividing the room, and hiding a portion of each side of the bar from this angle. I feel certain Savage and Smith can see us, even if we can't see them. I reach for the glass, planning to sip lightly. "Thank you."

"When are you getting married?" he asks.

"Saturday."

Now *his* brows lift. "This Saturday?"

"Yes," I confirm. "So the nerves and excitement have kicked in."

"Who's the lucky guy?" He sips from his glass and that ring catches my eye.

I have no idea why but his question feels uncomfortable. "He's in high-end security," I reply, not willing to offer Rick's name. "Do you have any more questions about the museum plans I've created?"

"You're talented," he states. "I'm curious. Do you design private homes?"

"My work is commercial only," I say, but even as I do, I have a flashback to my call with Savage and the drawings I'd created afterward. *"We should buy a place in the Hamptons. We can escape up there, just you and me. What do you think?"* I sip my wine to suppress my smile before I say, "I want to be the best at what I do and I feel specializing allows me that ability."

"What if I agreed to fund the museum wing, but as a condition, you design a home for me? A paid job for you, of course."

"I'd say I'm flattered, but I'm not comfortable being a part of that negotiation."

"You already are or you wouldn't be meeting with me."

"I can recommend someone talented—"

"I want you."

There is something in the way he says those words that sit all kinds of wrong. "I'm flattered, and I hope to hear great news about the museum. I'd be honored to create something special to honor your father."

He studies me for several beats and while his stare is unreadable, my face under his attention feels inappropriate. I wonder if Savage is watching. I'm sure he is, and I don't think he would like how Kirk is looking at me. And Lord help Kirk if I don't end this now.

"I should get home," I say quickly. "A bride-to-be needs her beauty sleep."

"Right," he says. "I believe Robin took care of our bill. I'll be in touch with her tomorrow. Can I walk you out or offer you a ride somewhere?"

"No. Thank you. I have a car service. I'll finish my wine while he pulls around."

His eyes linger on my face and then he gives a small nod and walks away. I'm left unsettled. And yes, he may have inappropriate intentions, but it feels like more than that. There is something that just felt off about him and the entire meeting. The moment he's out of sight, I stand, and hurry toward the bar, ready to be with my very large, very protective, soon-to-be husband.

LISA RENEE JONES

CHAPTER SEVENTEEN

Candace

The minute I'm at the giant pillar to my left, Rick is placing me against it, planting his hands on either side of me. "What the hell was that?"

"Uncomfortable," I say, "but I handled it."

"I was about twenty seconds from handling it."

Smith eyes me over a barstool to my left behind Rick. "I was here in case I had to save the guy's life."

"Seriously, Candace," Rick says. "What the fuck was that?"

I shift away from the pole and wrap my arms around him. "Can we just go home?"

"Candace, damn it—"

I push to my toes and kiss him, a quick brush of lips, before I say, "I know you trust me to handle myself or tell you I need help. And right now, I really need to just be with you. I'll tell you all about it later. When we feel up to talking."

His eyes heat and he leans in low and close, his lips at my ear, and says, "We talk first, baby, because once we're naked, the only words I want from you are 'Please, Rick. More, Rick.'"

I laugh and push him back. "Let's go home."

He strokes a lock of hair behind my ear. "I will never get tired of hearing you say those words."

My heart swells. "Home means more now. You know?"

"You know I do."

He captures my hand and rotates to Smith. "We're outta here. Thanks for taking care of her. Now go find some company for the night. Ashley was never the woman for you. And she married another man. Who she loves, Smith."

"Fuck off, Savage."

He releases me and walks over to Smith and leans in close, murmuring something for his ears only before he returns to me. His arm slides around my shoulders and sets us in motion. On our way home.

Finally.

But as happy as I am about Rick being home, I'm sad for Smith. I know what being alone and in love is like. I want him to find his happiness, too.

Once we're at the front door, about to head out into the cold night air, I slip into my coat. "Brr," I say. "Hello, winter night."

"Stay inside where it's warm. I'll have them pull the car up." He kisses me and heads outside with long, ridiculously masculine strides. Since the moment I met him, that way about him—that explosive raw alpha energy—has always done it for me. Because beneath all of that, he's complicated, layers upon layers of complicated. And yet, I understand him like he's another part of me. He *is* another part of me.

I draw in a breath on the sensation of being watched and fight the urge to turn and look around. Instead, I walk to the side of one of the doors and pretend to lean on the wall, scanning my surroundings, but no one and nothing stands out. Why am I having this feeling when Rick is home? I thought I was just paranoid about his little mission. Apparently, it's more than that.

Savage reappears in the lobby, scanning for me, and I call out his name. "Over here."

He motions me forward and offers me his hand. I hurry forward and accept it, but plant my feet. "Before we leave, I know this is crazy, but last night I felt like I was being watched. I told Blake. But I feel it again. Maybe I'm having wedding jitters and it's making me lose my mind. Can we just elope already?"

He cups my neck and drags my mouth to his, kisses me, and says, "Never ignore a gut feeling. And Blake told me what happened." He snakes his phone from his pocket and punches in a number. "Smith," he says. "You still here?" He listens a minute and then says, "Good. Candace feels like she's being watched again." He listens again and then says, "Really? Ain't that something, man. Thanks." He disconnects.

"He says Kirk never left the hotel. He just walked back into the bar. I don't know who you felt watching you last night, but after the way that fucktard was looking at you at the table, he's our suspect tonight."

"I don't know if it's him," I say, "but," I slide my hand into his, "I want to go home."

"So I shouldn't find the fucktard, beat the fucktard, and make him wish he was never born before we leave?"

"No," I say precisely. "You should not. Take me home and undress me."

"Well," he says, "since you put it that way."

He slides his arm around me, leads me out of the hotel, and helps me into the fancy new BMW 5 series he bought last month. And once he's inside, behind the wheel, I'm not thinking of being watched by anyone but him.

CHAPTER EIGHTEEN

Candace

The car is warm from the heater, the spicy scent of Rick's cologne teasing my nostrils and stirring my senses, but not wiping away my concerns.

Once we're on the road, I rotate in my seat to study him, the streetlights cutting through the darkness, his chiseled jaw set tight. It's a dead giveaway that all is not well, but then, I'd already figured that out. "What happened?" I ask, getting straight to the point.

"I went in, *the big bad boss*, and got it done. And here I am." He shoots me a look, his lips curved slightly, and gives me a little wink.

From the day I met this man, he's always used charm and jokes, among other methods of distraction, to protect himself and shelter others. But in doing so, he pushes people away. He should know that doesn't work with me.

"Rick," I press softly but firmly.

He draws a breath, turns a corner, and then casts me a look. "It didn't go perfectly," he says, his tone serious now. "But I'm home."

"What does 'it didn't go perfectly' mean?"

His cellphone rings. He reaches for it and I say, "Don't answer it. Not until you tell me what happened."

He glances at the screen and then me and says, "I need to take this," before he punches the answer button and greets his caller with "Yeah, man." He listens a minute. "And?" He's silent again. "No." His tone darkens. "I *said no*." He hangs up and pulls the car to the front of our building, places it in park, and glances at me. "Let's go upstairs."

I don't push. Not now. Something is going on and it's not good. And I don't even care about the timing just before our wedding. I care about Rick's safety. The doorman opens my door, and I step outside into the chill of the night that is somehow chillier with the impact of tonight's events. Rick is instantly right beside me, his big body sheltering mine from the wind. Which would be wonderful if it wasn't so completely symbolic of all the ways his need to shelter me has destroyed us in the past.

I tell myself this is now. The past is the past. He hands off the keys to the doorman and says, "If you play, you pay. It's not always worth it, either."

The doorman, a young kid I've never seen before, blanches, and looks confused. Savage laughs, and throws his arm around me, setting us in motion. He enjoys his witchery of words that fuck with people's heads, but somewhere in the depth of everything he says is a little piece of brilliance. And often, something not as gentle as it may seem, something dark. We enter the building, and I decide it's almost as if he'd been talking to himself, not the kid.

"You play, you pay?" I ask, glancing up at him.

"Wise words from a man who hasn't been wise," he assures me, leaning in and kissing me before he punches the elevator button.

And I have my confirmation.

You play, you pay holds meaning.

One I'm no doubt going to understand soon.

Once we're inside the elevator, he gives me no chance to ask the questions I need to ask. He keys in our floor and then his hand is under my hair, his palm against my skin, stealing my breath a moment before his mouth lowers just above mine, his breath a warm tease that promises a kiss. And I *want* that kiss. God, how I want it.

"I missed you," he says, his voice a low rasp of emotion. "So damn much."

"I missed you, too," I whisper, and then his lips press to mine and I'm leaning into him, into the moment, into the slide of his tongue. Warmth spreads through me as I taste the two sides of Rick I know so well—the tenderness of a man who loves me, and the demand, the dominance, of a man with too much to ever forget, but he tries.

The elevator dings and his mouth parts from mine, but there is a reluctance there I so understand. "Come on," he says, capturing my hand and guiding me out of the car and into the hallway. Suddenly, that pay-for-play and a need for answers aren't on my mind. My nipples are puckered. My skin is hot. Dampness clings to my thighs. We need each other right now. That's what matters. Rick opens the door and urges me inside, but he's right there behind me. He locks up, secures the entryway with the comprehensive security system he'd installed long before I moved in with him, and I don't miss the fact that this isn't a step that he misses. Not that he ever does, but I feel some sense of necessity in the action tonight.

I start to find a need for logic and information again. It pierces the haze of lust and love and I step further into the apartment, about to find distance from Rick to allow me to think. I can't think when he's touching me. But I'm too late with my escape. Rick catches my hand and pulls me around to him, folds me close, strokes the hair from my face, and tilts my gaze to his. "I just need you right now, okay?"

"What happened to talking first?"

"It was never going to happen. You know, Candy, baby, when I came off of a shit-show of a few days, and I didn't have you, I drank. Now, I don't drink. I want to fuck you and make love to you. In that order. Maybe all at once."

I melt with that confession, words I needed to hear for so many years, when there was nothing but silence. I tremble inside with how much I love this man. How much I still feel the pain of losing him even when he's standing right in front of me—some part of me always thinks I'll lose him again. I push to my toes and press my lips to his. And he cups my head and slants his mouth over mine, and kisses me like I'm the only reason he can breathe.

"I do very little properly," he says softly. "You know that, right?"

I laugh and stroke my fingers over his jaw, the rasp of multiple days of stubble teasing my fingers. "I like that about you. You know that, right?"

"I do, but let's make at least one thing proper about tonight. I haven't been in our bed with you in way too fucking long." He scoops me up and starts walking toward the stairs.

CHAPTER NINETEEN

Candace

Rick enters the bedroom where moonlight spills into the room from the floor-to-ceiling windows, stars twinkling in the clear night sky. He sets me on my feet at the end of the bed. "Undress for me," he says, rotating me as he sits on the bed, his hands on my hips.

In that moment, I flash back to the first time Rick ever said those words to me. *Undress for me.*

It's been one month since we met. And we've been together every moment we weren't working. I open the door to find Rick standing there, looking like sin and my satisfaction, in jeans that hug his powerful lower body and a snug T-shirt, that accents his defined biceps, his hand over his head on the doorframe, and one look at his face— his steely jaw, his dark eyes—I know something is wrong.

"Come in," I say, and when I back-up to allow him to enter, he steps inside and shuts the door.

A moment later, he pulls me into his arms, and kisses me until my knees are weak, a dark kiss. A tormented kiss. I press my hand to his jaw. "I think you need a drink."

"I need a lot of things right now," he confesses, and for a man who'd thus far confessed very little to me, it feels like a breakthrough.

I catch his hand and lead him to the couch, and once he sits down, I head into the kitchen and pour him a drink, a specific whiskey I've come to know he enjoys. I don't pour one for me. I'm just not a good enough drinker to drink and be a good listener.

I return to the living room to find his elbows on his knees, his head low. I sit next to him and when he offers me a dark stare, I offer him the glass. He accepts it, sips it, and sets it down, uninterested, it seems.

"What happened?" I ask.

"I'm trouble for you, Candace," he says, holding that eye contact. "I'm trouble and I'm not a relationship guy."

My heart thunders to a roar in my chest and my defense mechanisms kick in. My hands slide down my legs and I stand up. He's on his feet in an instant and we face each other. My hand is trembling and I hate how obviously flustered I am. My heart is breaking, which is ridiculous. I've only known him for a month. But my voice is remarkably firm. "You didn't have to come here to tell me you don't want to see me again. I haven't asked for a commitment."

"And you shouldn't," he says, confusing me.

I blanch. "What?"

He steps into me, folds me close, his big, hard body overwhelming me in what I call all the right ways if that confusion I'm feeling wasn't so damn ripe. "I had a shit day today," he says. "Real shit. The kind I keep to myself. The kind I don't want to bring into your life. And yet, I found myself on your doorstep. I found myself needing to be here with you."

"You're confusing me, Rick."

He releases me and steps back, running a rough hand through his hair. "You just won't let me go."

"What? You came here to me. I don't want someone who doesn't want me."

"I want you, Candace. I want you more than you possibly know. But I'm trying to protect you."

"I can protect myself."

"Really? My father's a bastard who beats my mother. He's drunk half the time and he's unfit to operate, but he does. And I haven't stopped him. That shit is my baggage. And tonight, I took over one of his surgeries. I forced him out and threatened to get him disbarred." He scrubs his jaw and says, "I need to go."

SAVAGE ENDING

My heart leaps and I rush after him, reaching him just in time to plant myself between him and the door, my hand landing on his chest, where his heart thunders madly.

"Why would you leave?"

"I told you. To protect you."

I swallow hard and say, "So you're breaking up with me?"

"Yes," he says, but there is a rasp in his voice.

"Okay. But you're here now. You came here because you need me. And Rick," my throat goes dry thinking of my mother being—gone forever. "I need you, too. So if it's only tonight—"

He cups my face and says, "I can't do one night with you. I've already proven that. It's all or nothing."

"And what do you want?"

"What do you want, Candace?"

I hesitate, but it's one of those all-in questions that requires an all-in answer. "All. Without question."

"And what if you can't handle it all, Candace?"

"My mother once told me that the bravest thing you can do is to trust someone with your heart. Trust me. I trust you."

"Do you?" he challenges.

"Yes," I say. "I do."

His lips lower, lingering above mine, his breath a hot fan, his emotions a stormy eruption, seeping inside me. I can't breathe. I can't move. I want him to kiss me, but he doesn't. He scoops me up and carries me to the bedroom. He turns on the light, leaving me no shelter in the darkness. And then he sets me down at the end of the mattress, him standing with his back to the foot of the bed. "Undress for me," he orders softly, and there is no question this is a command.

But it's one that comes with a choice. He sits down and makes it clear in that action that he wants to watch. It's hard to explain how intense it is to have a man like Rick Savage watching you with this kind of stormy intensity and dominance, but it's consuming. My mind goes back to moments before when I'd said I trusted him. And he'd said, prove it.

I've sensed this darker sexual side to Rick, a dominant side, that for all my independence, appeals to me in ways I never expected. I like it. And I probably love him. Perhaps because he's careful not to demand, but rather ask, in every other way of our relationship. Some might call whatever this is lust, but I don't think so. Either way, I seem to understand him at a soul-deep level. He dominates right now. And he wants me to trust him. He wants me to be willing to be vulnerable with him, even after his confessions tonight. Especially because of those confessions.

And so, I do it.

Nervous, excited, aroused, I toe off my shoes, slip out of my pants, and tear away my T-shirt and bra. And when I stand there, fully naked, he doesn't come closer. He just stares at me, his gaze a hot wash of heat as he inspects every part of me. And when he stands and walks toward me, my nipples are hard and my thighs slick. I ache for the touch that follows. His hands cup my neck over my hair and he drags me to him. "You do know that I'm not even close to done with all I want from you tonight, don't you?"

"I certainly hope not," I whisper.

And his lips curve, with satisfaction I don't fully understand, but I want to. God, how I want to.

I return to the present, and I know this is a night when Rick Savage, needs to be in control. And he needs to know that I trust him no matter what. I undress for him, and this time, my hands still tremble, and my heart still races. Because I know what comes next.

CHAPTER TWENTY

Candace

I stand willingly in front of Rick, naked while he is not. His gaze is hot, intimate. When his eyes meet mine, he says, "You hesitated."

"I did *not* hesitate," I say, closing the space between us and pressing my hand to his jaw. "I was thinking about the very first time you told me to undress for you. Do you remember?"

Tension slides from his shoulders as if my answer is the exact answer he needs, and he wraps his arms around my waist. "I remember that night well." His voice lowers seductively. "I spanked you." His lips curve. "And you liked it."

"Are you going to spank me now?" I dare, so far from intimidated by anything that happens between me and this man. He demands. And I have learned over time that while it defies my strong will and independence in the bedroom, I like when he's in control.

"Not tonight," he says, easing me onto his lap so I'm straddling him.

I wrap my arms around his neck and he adds, "All or nothing."

"All or nothing," I repeat.

His lashes lower, the lines of his face sharp. "I'm still Savage, Candace," he says, his eyes meeting mine again. "That part of me still exists."

"Why are you saying this?" I ask.

"Because this mission, this blast from the past, reminded me of who I am."

"And you think I need to be reminded?"

"Yes," he says without hesitation. "You do. You're about to marry me."

"I'm marrying the love of my life. And that's you, Rick. All of you."

"Love is blind."

"I know who you are, Rick Savage. And for the record, you can't deny who you are. Not and live a happy life. And I don't want you to deny who you are. That's never been my message."

"I know that, too," he says. "But I've tried anyway."

That one statement terrifies me. *I've tried anyway.* It's like a ball rolling toward a waterfall in slow motion, but eventually, it tumbles over the edge. My hands go to his shoulders, his muscles flexing beneath my touch. "That's a problem for us. It's a big problem."

I try to climb off of him, but he catches my waist with a powerful arm around my body. "It's not a problem," he insists.

"No one should marry someone they can't be themselves with. Every time you think you have to be something you're not for me, it divides us."

"I don't want to be something I'm not with you, Candace. I want to be a better *man* for you."

"I just want you to be *you.*"

"I want to be a better man for me, too. But you know, sometimes some people just need to die, Candace."

I blink with the sudden shift from being a better man to wanting to kill someone. But that's the point of all of this. That's where he was taking me and us.

I'm flying blind right now, unsure about what happened to place him in this state of mind, but I know one thing: Rick is a good man. He doesn't kill for money or pleasure. "I love you, Rick *Savage.* Be who you are and do what you do for the right reasons. And you do. Always."

"Even if it means hunting down a bastard and killing him?"

He says it so matter-of-factly, but I know him. It's anything but. Someone, Max, I suspect, has made Rick's personal hit list. There are no names on that list, at least, none that are living. "Can it be after the honeymoon?" I ask, quite seriously.

He laughs and cups my head and presses our foreheads together. "You really get me, don't you?"

My hand finds his face. "And you get me. Rick—"

I never finish my sentence. I don't even remember what I was going to say. He pulls me closer and claims my mouth, and it's a tender kiss, a kiss void of the dominance I'd expected from him only minutes before. His hand slides up and down my back and around to my breast, his fingers teasing my nipple. I moan with the sensations that spiral through me and just that easily, the air shifts, and our mood darkens, roughens. Suddenly, we are wild, kissing as if we will never again. Touching each other everywhere, and I'm tugging at his shirt. He pulls it over his head and tosses it, and my gaze falls on the heart that says San Antonio in the center, the heart I know he got for me. Because that's where we met, that's where he left me and found me again.

My fingers curl on top of it and I whisper, "You really never forgot me."

"Never," he says, and as our eyes collide, he says it again, a rasp of emotion in his voice. "*Never.*" And then he's kissing me and I'm touching him and arching into him, the thick ridge of his erection between my thighs.

We shift and I stroke the front of his jeans, tugging at his zipper. "I can't get it," I breathe out, anxious, frenzied. He stands up and takes me with him, and I don't know when he took his boots off, but *thank God*, they are gone. We get rid of the rest of his clothing all that much easier. And when he's naked, my hand eagerly wraps the thick pulse of his jutting cock. His hand covers mine and a low rough sound rolls from deep in his broad chest. He picks me up. My legs wrap around his hips, my arms holding onto his neck and he walks to his side of the bed, sitting on the mattress and taking me with him. I know he intends to move to the headboard, but it doesn't happen.

The hard length of him presses to my backside, and I press into him and we're kissing and touching until he falls backward onto the mattress with me on top of him, hands pressed to his shoulders. "Rick," I say and then I add, "*Savage.*"

He rolls me over onto my back, fitting his big, powerful body over mine, his erection thick between my legs, holding my hands to the side of my head with his hands. "Don't call me that," he says. "Rick. You call me Rick."

"You don't get to be one person with me and another with everyone else. Be Savage. He turns me on. And I happen to love him."

His lashes lower, his jaw set tight, his face skyward, turbulence radiating from him before he fixes me in an intense stare. Still holding my hands, he leans in, inhaling my scent, a floral perfume I know he loves. His lips brush my ear as he says, "What are you doing to me and us, woman?"

"Making sure forever means forever."

He stares at me with those intense eyes that I imagine pierce an enemy's soul as surely as they do mine. He doesn't speak, but he leans in closer and nuzzles my neck. His lips brush the delicate skin there. He kisses it, the sensation hot and warm, and my nipples pucker. His lips tease a delicious path over my jaw to my lips where they linger as he says, "I have no intention of losing you, again. Whatever I have to do to protect you and us, I will."

I know immediately that his reply references whatever is going on with this Max situation. It's not over. But his mouth is back on my neck, and this time it travels lower, until his tongue is lapping at my nipples. Unable to touch him, I arch my back and he suckles hard enough that I feel the sweet ache all the way down my body to clench my sex.

As if he knows just how much I need him inside me, his shaft slides along the wet, sensitive seam of my body, and then he's inside me. I pant out several breaths with the feel of him stretching me, and when he releases my hands, my fingers dive into his hair. He rolls us to our sides, facing each other, his hands on my ass. And when he thrusts, hard and deep, he gives me a hard smack and then squeezes my backside. I gasp and laugh. And he says, "I didn't want you to miss the spanking."

I laugh breathlessly. "So generous of you."

He nips my lips, an erotic love bite, and then we're just breathing together, the air shifting, thickening. Our bodies sway—a slow, seductive dance that burns with a deep, burning need. Soon we're moving more intensely, our kisses passionate, our touches almost frenzied. I want to slow down. I want to make this last, but the ache in my body just won't listen. I press into Rick, fingers tangling roughly in his hair, and he answers with the same. He captures my hair and gently tugs my head backward, his teeth scraping my neck. His cock is thrusting deep, and then he's rolling me to my back again, thrusting again and again, and I'm at the point of no return. He lifts my knee and presses it to his chest, drives into me again, and I shatter, my sex clenching and then going into spasms.

Still, he drives into me, and every muscle in my body screams *yes, more.* Keep going. And just when I'm coming down, when I'm on the other side of the orgasm, he groans, his head tilted back with the intensity of his release. He shudders, shakes, and with another deep, guttural moan, collapses, catching his weight on his arms above me.

Long seconds pass, his head buried in the crook of my neck, before he pulls out of me and rolls to his back. "You destroy me in all the right ways, woman," he says, glancing over at me.

I smile, pleased with this reaction but it fades almost instantly. There's more to that statement, a reverse effect. He's always believed he'd one day destroy me in all the wrong ways. I curl up next to his side and say, "You don't destroy me, Rick Savage. You save me every single day."

CHAPTER TWENTY-ONE

Savage

You save me every single day.

Candace's words slide inside me and stir love, devotion, and self-hate for leaving her alone and exposed in the past, no matter what my good intentions. Proof that she makes me human when not so long ago, I wasn't sure I was anymore.

Candace touches my cheek and then kisses my jaw. "I'm going to the bathroom," she announces before scooting off the bed, grabbing my shirt, and walking naked toward the bathroom while pulling it over her head. I'm like a kid in a candy store with this woman in my life. And I love the fuck out of her in my shirt. I love the fuck out of *her*. And it's my job as her future husband to protect her. That doesn't seem like a simple thing.

I save her every day.

Bullshit.

She saves me.

And I will not let anything happen to her.

Ever.

I stand up, and grab my jeans, pulling them on but not bothering to zip them up. The moon hovers low in the sky, and I walk to the window to stare at it, reminded of a night years ago in Mexico where just such a moon led me from the cartel-infested jungle to safety. I called it my magic moon that spoke to me without one single word. Well, damn it, give me some magic now. Talk to me now. Tell me how to protect Candace and not lie to her. Tell me how to be honest with her and not ruin the wedding for her. For long minutes, that's the battle I fight within myself.

Suddenly, Candace is beside me, pressing close to my side, all soft and sweet, her hand settling on my belly. "Hey," she whispers.

Time's up.

The truth or a lie.

The time of decision has come.

I turn to her, hands on her tiny waist, and pull her to me. "Hey, future Mrs. Savage."

She smiles, and damn, she has an angel's smile. I can't lie to her, no matter how good my intentions. Good intentions haven't served me well with Candace. I have never lied to her. I won't start now.

"That's me," she says, "and I can't wait to be Mrs. Savage." Her fingers brush my jaw. "You haven't shaved since you left. You're about a beard instead of a goatee. You should let me shave you."

I capture her fingers and kiss them. "Tomorrow." My hands settle on her shoulders. "We should talk."

"You're very serious right now. And considering you are you, that feels rather ominous."

"Only because I dread telling you anything that isn't perfect right before our wedding. And I considered not telling you what I'm going to tell you at all, not until after the wedding, but that's not who I want us to be."

"But you want to protect me," she supplies.

"Hell yes, I want to protect you, Queen Candace."

She laughs. "Queen Candace? That's new. And that makes you king, right?"

"Was that ever a question?" I tease, but I'm already leading her toward the couch and the coffee table, where there's a bottle of wine and two glasses, that at one point, a few days back before I left for Tennessee, we meant to drink and never touched.

We sit and I reach for the bottle and open it. And while I'm pouring, she studies my magic moon. "It's beautiful," she says, "so close, and yet so far away." Her gaze shifts and she angles in my direction, her eyes meeting mine as she adds, "A bit like our wedding."

I hand her a glass. "Nothing will stop us from getting married if that's what you're afraid of."

"I don't know what happened when you were away. But I wish you would have said no to Max."

I sip from the glass I've filled for myself. "I wish it were that simple." I draw in a breath and shake my head. "I'm not sure this situation is what it seems. And I'm not sure it wouldn't have ended up on our doorstep no matter what."

"What does that mean?" she asks. "I mean, Tag is dead. And I thought Max was your friend."

I set my glass down and she does the same with hers before we face each other and both settle a leg on the couch between us. "Max wanted me to grab a data drive and drop it at another location. Simple. Easy. Fast. Except we got to the pick-up location, and there were a group of men waiting."

Her eyes go wide. "For you? Were they waiting for you?"

"One could assume so. Now did they want what I was after or did they just want me dead? I can't say. And neither can they. We killed them all."

"My God," she whispers. "What else?"

"Max stopped taking my calls. I had no way to make the drop he wanted me to make. I hid it on the property where I was supposed to make the drop. That way if he calls, I can tell him where it is."

"I thought you were taking him money after the drop?" she asks.

"We got to his cabin in Colorado to do just that and there was no Max. The cabin was in disarray, a cup of coffee shattered on the ground. Someone was there and left. Again, one can assume it was Max."

"Okay. But if Max set you up, surely he wouldn't have given you the right address to find him."

I blink. "So did Max set you up or was he set-up?" Candace asks.

"I'd like to think Max is a good guy—he saved my life— but I can't make that work in my head. How did those men that attacked us know when and where to go if he didn't tell them?"

"So obviously you found the data drive. Did you look at it? What was on it?"

It's a question I'd hoped she wouldn't ask because it tells a story, and it's not a good one. "A list of five locations." I hesitate, but I decide I can't hold back. "And all five locations are places I did jobs with Max."

"Oh God," she says again, and then she goes exactly where I knew she'd go next. "This is about you. You kept insurance on all your hits. Could he have stolen that insurance? Could he be using it to blackmail someone? Could he have blamed you when the situation went south?"

It's exactly where my head is, but I don't want to fuel her worry. "Don't turn this into an earthquake when it's a thunderstorm."

"Should you have delivered the drive if it connects to you?"

"As I told Asher and Adam, I might have been drunk back then, but not stupid. I didn't hide anything in the places Max thinks I hid them. Maybe he went behind me and hid his own insurance. But if he gambled on a fact that wasn't a fact, that's on him,"

"That answer feels like trouble," she says. "What did you say no to on the phone and to whom?" she asks.

"Asher wanted me to come and look at the data he pulled on the guys who attacked us. I wasn't going anywhere until I saw you."

"You need to go see Asher," she urges.

"Tomorrow morning."

"Now," she insists. "We have a few days until we get married, Rick" She tries to stand, and I catch her hand. "We need to go now," she argues.

"I've barely slept in three days. Let's go to bed."

"Rick, we need—"

My cellphone rings and halts her words. Out of necessity, I snake it from my pocket and glance at the caller ID. The number is unknown. I show it to Candace and answer the line. "Who is this?"

"Max," comes a rough familiar voice. "It's Max. Tell me you got the data drive."

"Well, what do you know?" I say, glancing at Candace and mouthing "Max" before I stand up and continue. "The big, fat, lying elephant in the room." I walk to the window. "Or maybe it's the slimy, slithering snake in the grass. I know it's hard to believe, but I was just fucking thinking about you, like really thinking about what I want to do to you. I won't keep you guessing. The story ends this way. You die."

"You think I set you up."

"I was ambushed by a bunch of losers in black who wanted to go to a funeral, Max, my man. Fucktard, pencil dick, this seems crystal clear. You were the only one who knew where I was."

"I told no one," he insists. "And they found me, too. I did everything right and they found me, too. If you went by the cabin, you know that."

"You used my hidden insurance to blackmail someone," I say and it's not a question. "Who?"

"Do you really want to know?"

"I'm going to pretend you didn't ask that because you resemble a drunk two-year-old when you ask stupid questions. They came after me. I want to know who I'll be killing next, besides you."

"Stop being a prick."

"You first," I say. "But then it's too late for you, now isn't it?"

"Where's the data drive?"

"We both know I looked on that drive, Max. It has five locations on it," I say. "You don't need the drive to relay that information."

"There is a map to each location. I need that map in the right hands."

"And I'm sure you have those memorized."

"Do you?"

He's reminding me I drank my way through those years. Bastard. "We're not talking about me. I'm not blackmailing someone with that information. Who are you blackmailing?"

"More like the opposite. I'm paying a debt just like you. Once it's paid, I'm free. And now you are too, from me."

"Who's blackmailing you then?"

"It's better you don't know."

"I'm involved. Not only am I your courier, I'm the one who buried those insurance policies."

"You're not the only one who buried a few secrets. And you don't want to know more. Give me the drop location. You're done afterward. We're even."

"I got ambushed," I remind him. "How the fuck am I not in this if I got ambushed? How did they know I was going to be there?"

"I texted you from what I thought was a safe burner. Obviously, I overused that phone. But yours was scrambled. I know yours was scrambled. No one can find you from that conversation. And I'm guessing anyone who saw you at the pick-up location is dead. You're out of this, man. Just give me the drop location and forget this happened."

A part of me wants to push. Another wants this to just be over. He's given me answers. Ones I'd hypothesized. Reasonable answers. And he's a loose cannon. You burn him. He burns you back. "X marks the spot in the woods behind the warehouse location you gave me," I say, and finish with the coordinates.

He hangs up.

That's a good response. It means that's what he wanted. And now he's gone.

I turn to face Candace and she's already closing the space between us, her hands catching my waist, urgency in her words as she says, "What just happened?"

My hands close down on her arms and I pull her to me. "It's over," I say, and I mean those words, despite the fact that they don't quite sit right on my tongue. "And now the past is the past. And we are the future."

And before she can ask another question, I scoop her up and get her naked and in the bed with me, where she belongs. Forever.

CHAPTER TWENTY-TWO

Savage

Candace and I order takeout from our favorite sub shop, and while we're waiting on the delivery, she heads to the bathroom to do all her nightly girl stuff. I head downstairs to wait for the food and use the opportunity to dial Asher.

"Savage, man," he answers. "Hold tight. I'm at Blake's place. Let me put him on speaker."

Ten seconds later, I hear, "What the fuck trouble are you getting yourself into right before your wedding, asshole?"

One thing I've always respected about Blake is his eloquent way with words, but I'll compliment him another day. Right now, I get to the point. "Max called," I begin before I proceed to deliver a quick rundown of the conversation.

There're a few beats of silence when I finish and some murmurs between Blake and Asher, before Asher says, "His explanation sounds reasonable, but we both agree it all sits uneasy, like about half a pizza too much. Let us do some digging around. Can you come by the office at lunchtime tomorrow?"

"Yeah," I say. "I'll be there."

And right when I would hang up, Blake adds, "We've got your back. If this has to be handled, we'll handle it for you. *You* are going to let it go and *get married* and then go on that honeymoon in Sonoma your wife-to-be has been ranting on and on about. That's an order from all of us here at Walker Security. Another order, this one from me. Get some rest."

He hangs up.

I let his message sink in and come to the obvious conclusion. Once again, and over and over, the Walker team teaches me the meaning of family.

For the first time in my life, I'm ready to hand over the shit-show rather than deal with it myself. I *want* to enjoy our wedding. And he's right. Candace is so damn excited about the California wine country and whale watching for our honeymoon. Hell, so am I.

The doorbell rings and I set aside all the bullshit, determined to unwind. A few minutes later, Candace and I are on the bed, opening the takeout bags. She's delectable in a red silk gown with just enough cleavage to bring me to my knees.

"I need you to put on a robe, my little bombshell babe. I can't eat the sandwich and you at the same time."

"Stop, Rick," she chides, "You're crazy."

"I'm as serious as a Jedi with a blue lightsaber. Robe. You *need* a robe."

She scowls and sets her sandwich down. "I cannot believe you are making me do this," she says, standing and walking toward the bathroom.

Her ass looks just as good as her breasts in that gown. I stand up and follow her. She has the robe in her hand when I catch her to me and toss it to the ground. "Our food," she objects, but her laughter weakens the objection.

I'm not laughing. I'm serious as fuck about getting her out of that gown. I pull it over her head, toss it to the ground, and lift her to the counter, her pretty pink nipples puckering with the cold air. I catch them with my fingers and she gasps, her lips parting and lifting in invitation. An invitation happily accepted. This is the point when she stops fighting and goes all-in on the idea of me inside her, right here and now. I know this because she tells me.

"Can you be inside me already?" she whispers.

"What about the food?" I tease.

"Rick, damn it." She tugs at my shirt.

I kiss her hard and fast and then I pull it over my head and by the time it's on the floor, she's unzipped my pants.

I shove them down, cup her backside with one hand, and slide my fingers along the slick seam of her sex with the other. She is wet and ready, and damn, I missed this part of us when we were apart, but then, I missed everything about us. I slide inside her and she arches her hips, her sex squeezing me, her lashes lowering, unbridled pleasure sliding over her beautiful face. She says I'm crazy. She's driving me crazy. And so, I drive into her and pick her up at the same time, and then we're rocking together, all fast and furious, but none of it is enough. It never is with Candace. My hand splays between her shoulder blades. "Lean back," I order, and she does. She trusts me to hold onto her when some might say I don't deserve her trust. I left her. I hurt her. I didn't hold onto her. I'll never make that mistake again.

I thrust hard and she presses into me, her beautiful breasts bouncing with every move. Just like they did in my fantasies all those years I couldn't let her go, I couldn't even begin to replace her. I have no hope of lasting. I don't even try. She moans loudly, this soft, sexy sound, and her sex clenches me hard and fast. I'm done. I thrust one more wicked time, and shudder into release.

When my body settles and she leans forward, into me, I set her on the counter. "Wear the robe."

She laughs and I pull out of her, then hand her a towel, followed by the robe. "I'll wear the robe."

I lift her off the counter and I'm glad I told her everything about the Max situation.

We're good.

We're better than good.

I'm not fucking that up.

LISA RENEE JONES

CHAPTER TWENTY-THREE

Savage

Candace and I end up back on the bed, eating our sandwiches and talking about the wedding and the honeymoon while we eat.

Afterward, exhaustion wins.

With Candace pressed against me, the shade covering up that magic moon, I fall asleep, and I sleep hard. I wake with Candace still close, the room dark, the clock reading six AM. With the cobwebs of exhaustion now gone, I replay the conversation with Max. Why couldn't he just have given the location of the drive to the person he was handing it over to? Maybe he didn't want the owner of the cabin to get hurt, I decide. Why didn't he pick it up himself? Maybe he knew they were onto him. He was afraid to make a move and endanger his wife. But where the hell *is* his wife? Was she with him at the cabin?

With all these things bothering me, I slip out of the bed, pull the blankets over Candace, and watch her snuggle into my pillow. She's content. She feels safe with me, because of me. I'm never letting that change. What I will do is let her sleep, and I do. I head into the bathroom to shower, shave, and dress. By the time I exit the bathroom, it's only seven and Candace is still sound asleep. Once I'm downstairs, I start the coffee. Then I grab some egg whites and mix up a couple of omelets to throw on when Candace wakes up.

In the meantime, I think.

About Max.

About who he'd blackmail with that insurance I'd kept.

About the past, and Tag, and all the piggies that said "wee wee wee" for him.

But more so, I think of all the big shots in the government that Tag worked for. People with a lot to lose if that program were to be exposed. I grab a pad and pen and start writing down everything I remember about the mission locations. It's all foggy, but there were at least one of those big shots I know I documented in my insurance. He is now the former NSA director, Jacob Allen.

I grab my notebook and google him. He's started a business with Ned Walters, the CEO of one of the top tech firms in the world. Not working, I amend. Jacob now has a lot to lose.

"You're up early," Candace says, heading down the stairs, already dressed in black jeans and a pink T-shirt she bought from a gift store right after moving here. And like all proud tourists, it proudly reads, "I Love New York." Only it turns out that she really does. Enough to stay with me.

I shut the computer and walk to the stove. "How about omelets?"

"Yes, please," she says, setting her sketch pad down on the island and perking up. "And coffee." She walks to the counter behind me and grabs a cup. "Someone has had a few cups," she comments, noting the pot is now half empty. "I predict you will be wired today and that many a wickedly bad joke will follow."

"I'm never wicked about anything," I assure her. "I'm a perfect fucking angel."

She laughs. "God thinks so. You weren't struck down by lightning in the church."

"Ex-fucking-actly," I say.

She grins and joins me at the stove, helping to finish up the preparation of the omelets. We sit down at the island and dig in. "I got inspired." She slides her drafting pad in front of me. "That's an idea for a house with a porch. I know we were just talking. The Hamptons is expensive, but it was fun imagining something for us."

I glance down to find a design for a house and then look up at her. "We have shit tons of money, baby," I say because

I put her on my bank accounts months ago without any hesitation. She doesn't want my money. She has never been about money.

"Yes. It's an insane amount of money."

"That you don't spend."

She laughs and points at her notepad. "This suggestion would argue otherwise."

I wink. "Let's do it. We should call a realtor and look for some land."

"Really?"

Her voice has this hopeful lift. I want to turn hope into reality, which is why I say, "Hell yes. We both loved it when we stayed at Royce's place a few months back. And I've been telling you we need something we pick together. And we need a place that is just about us. An escape from everything."

"All right then." Hope sounds like excitement now. "I'll make some calls after the wedding. What's our budget?"

Her cellphone rings from the table where it rests, and she glances at the caller ID. "Robin," she says, grabbing it. "From the museum." She answers the call. "Hi, Robin." She listens a moment and then says, "That's great news." Another pause, and, "Today? You do know I'm getting married Saturday, right?" She listens a minute and then says, "Give me a moment." She hits mute and sighs. "The investor came through, but he won't write the check until I sign my contract."

"You want the project. It can't take that long." I study her a moment. "What's up, baby?"

"The investor said he wouldn't pay them unless I sign. I just get weird vibes from him."

"No worries. I'll wrap his legs around his head if needed. And once he signs the contract, it won't even matter."

She laughs. "My hero." She unmutes the phone and says, "It has to be quick. I have a final fitting today." Her and Robin talk back and forth, and she ends the call. "She wants to have lunch. I'm going to try to get out of that."

"I have to meet with Blake today at noon." I grab my phone and text Smith before I add, "I'm going to have one of the guys take you."

"I'll be fine on my own. It's daylight and I'll be with Robin."

My text messages ping and I glance down, before saying. "Smith is already confirmed."

She pushes off the stool and I rotate to allow her to step between my legs. "You're overly protective."

"Says the woman who's been feeling like she's been watched, and fending off the advances of some creepy rich guy. Which by the way, are always the most dangerous ones. They think they're entitled."

"I'll just shoot him if necessary," she says, her tone and expression serious, but then she smiles. "I think it might be less painful than you wrapping his legs around his neck."

"But I'll enjoy it less."

"You're crazy." She kisses me. "I need to go change." She hurries away and when she reaches the stairs she calls out, "Don't forget. Tomorrow morning you're going to Adam's place. And really, you should go tonight. It's bad luck to see the bride-to-be the day before the wedding." She turns and hurries up the stairs.

I want her cute little ass, but I hold my tongue.

I'm not going to go to Adam's place. Leaving Candace is bad luck.

CHAPTER TWENTY-FOUR

Candace

I choose an emerald green long-sleeved dress with black tights and boots for my meeting. Rick walks me downstairs and to the front of the building where Smith is waiting for me. Once I'm in the front seat of the SUV Smith is driving, Rick leans in and kisses me. "Tell Kirk the perv to keep his hands off of you," he orders.

My lips curve and I say, "Thankfully Kirk is not supposed to be at this meeting."

"Until he shows up." He leans down to eye Smith across my lap and says, "Keep her close or I'll kill you."

"I'm shaking in my boots," Smith replies dryly.

"As you should be," Rick assures him, but of course, he's just joking. Mostly, I think.

Rick kisses me again and then shuts me inside the vehicle with Smith.

"I think he wants me to keep you close," Smith says dryly.

"Ya think?" I tease.

A few minutes later, we arrive at the museum, and with my portfolio on my shoulder, just in case Robin wishes to review the designs, I walk into the museum's grand foyer.

The offices are upstairs and to the left, just past a giant dinosaur and several smaller ancient reptiles, and it's not long until I'm standing at Robin's office door. I peek inside her small but cozy office. Robin is indeed sitting behind her desk where it faces a wall, her gaze intently on a document, while bookshelves line the wall behind her.

I knock on the doorframe and her gaze jerks up and to me. She instantly pops to her feet. "You're here?! I'm so excited. Are you excited?" She motions to my dress and then hers, which is also emerald green, and laughs. "This is how on the same page we are. This was meant to be." She pats the arm of the guest chair next to her.

"It certainly seems that way," I agree as we both sit down. "I wanted this project in a bad way and you just never gave up."

"Honestly, I'm ashamed to tell you this, but I really had. Kirk called rather out of the blue and in a matter of days, here we are. As soon as I fax him your signed contract, he's giving us five million dollars." She slides the contract in front of me. "It's the exact contract you were ready to sign before the prior financing fell apart."

Yet another uneasy feeling slides down my spine and settles in my belly. "I'm curious. How did Kirk find out about the project?"

"Lucky us. He knows the prior investor who backed out. It just came together, as I said, like magic."

I'm not sure why this situation is bothering me, other than of course, his demand for my involvement. But he is spending five million dollars. Perhaps it's just a power play, him flexing a muscle to show he's in control. Maybe this is just the beginning.

"Is he planning to be involved on a day-to-day basis?"

"He's actually leaving town tonight, just as soon as we get your contract signed."

This should make me feel better. It doesn't.

"What's wrong?" she asks.

I shut her door.

"Oh God," she says. "You're backing out. Tell me you're not backing out."

"Not backing out, just treading forward with caution. Kirk was a little inappropriate last night. And he tried to hold me prisoner. He told me that if I didn't design his personal home, he wouldn't give you the money."

"Oh my. Oh no. Did you agree?"

"No. I don't do residential work and I don't intend to start for Kirk. I politely declined. I just need to know you can be the buffer between me and him."

"Of course I can, but I'm not sure what to do. I can't have someone working for the museum being sexually harassed."

"I'm not going down that rabbit hole," I assure her. "And I don't want your team, or the many contractors who will make a living off this, to suffer. I'd just like to limit my contact with Kirk."

"Are you sure?"

"I'm sure." I pick up the pen on the desk and flip to the signature page. "I'm passionate about this project." I sign the contract.

"Why am I not as excited as I was a few minutes ago?" she asks.

"Be excited. I am. But now I need to go. As you know, I have my final fitting."

"No lunch?"

"Right before I squeeze everything into that dress? Ah no. But we will have plenty of lunches coming up."

I stand and she follows me to my feet. "Thank you for coming so close to your wedding."

"You'll be there, right? I sent you an invitation."

"I will," she says. "I wouldn't miss it for the world."

"Me either," I joke.

We hug and I depart. I've made it to the giant dinosaur again when Kirk appears in my line of sight. My heart races and I have a moment where I consider hiding behind the dinosaur, but it's silly and ridiculous. I keep my pace and once we're standing in front of each other, he offers me his hand. I resist touching him, but force myself to accept his hand.

"Good to see you, again," he says, holding onto me a little too long. "I hope this means you signed the contract."

"I did," I say. "I'm thrilled you all had confidence in me."

"Your work is stunning," he assures me. "Enough so that I tried to bribe you to design my home, but I liked your backbone. That means you won't be convinced to deviate from what you believe will make this investment beautiful."

I blink, surprised by his reply. He was testing me? That's the gist, I think. "I'm the daughter of not one, but two military parents. I was taught to fight in every possible way." It's out before I can stop it, a warning that I am trained. I am capable of fighting back.

His eyes narrow, and there is a slight lift to the corners of his mouth that I cannot quite call a smile. More a smirk, I think.

"I have no doubt. I'm leaving town tonight. Can you spare time for lunch?"

"Sorry, no. Wedding preparations. But thank you. I can't wait to get started on the project."

"After the honeymoon, of course."

"Sorry, but yes," I say, but I'm not really sorry at all. "I can't wait."

"Where are you going?"

"Hawaii," I lie, and I don't know why. "Kauai."

"Well, have a fun and safe honeymoon." He gives a small bow, steps around me, and walks away.

I don't turn to watch him leave.

I rush for the door. I need out of here. And I don't think I breathe again until I'm in the vehicle with Smith.

"You okay?" he asks.

"Kirk was here," I say.

"I saw him walk in. What happened?"

I glance over at him. "Nothing bad, but he makes me uneasy. I lied to him about where Rick and I are honeymooning."

"You did good. Never ignore a gut feeling." He starts the engine. "To your fitting?"

I glance at the time on my cellphone. "Are you up for a bite to eat? I didn't want to go with Robin, and thank God, or I would have ended up with Kirk, too. But truly I'm starving and I have an hour to kill. Unless I have time to go to Walker and talk to Rick about Kirk?"

"Not in New York traffic. Blake is already checking out Kirk. And as for food, I'm up for a bite to eat. Always. Where?"

"Tacos?" I suggest.

"Taco Thursday. I love it." He sets us in action.

I settle into my seat and think about his words, which echo Blake's and Savage's "always trust your gut." I do. I just wish I understood what it's telling me.

LISA RENEE JONES

CHAPTER TWENTY-FIVE

Savage

Blake, Adam, and Asher are in the conference room gorging themselves on pizza when I arrive at the Walker offices. "I see Santa arrived early this year," I say, grabbing a slice and sitting down in front of an extra-large pepperoni pie, Adam's favorite. I give him a grin. "You don't mind sharing, right?"

"Would it matter?" he asks dryly.

"Good point," I say, glancing between Asher and Blake. "What else good is happening?"

"We checked out the investor in the museum," Blake says, sliding a file in my direction. "He looks legit."

"At least on the surface," Asher says. "All I did was run his basic info. If you want, I can dig deeper."

"It depends," I say, glancing at the billionaire bastard's profile and shutting the file again. "Aside from him wanting in my future wife's pants, is there any other reason I should kill him? Is there any chance he's connected to this bullshit with Max?"

"The guys who ambushed us were all ex-military, all working for some private for-hire security company," Asher says. "They were young. Too young to connect back to Tag or you and Max, but we checked for links anyway. Nothing showed up."

"What about a connection to Jacob Allen, the ex-NSA director?"

"I saw nothing that linked to anyone involved—Tag, Candace's father, or you," Blake says, and after he finishes off a slice of pizza adds, "And while Max tells you he's being blackmailed, I suspect it's the other way around. I can't prove that but my gut, based on what you've told me, is that he was looking for a payday. But the good news here is I can't find a link back to you. We've scoured the black web, made contact with informants in the right places, and we've come up with nothing."

"What about Max?" Adam asks for me. "Anything on him in all that digging around the web?"

"Nothing," Blake says.

I grimace. "Yeah well, that's like saying you didn't see Jack go up the hill with Jill, but he rolls down a few minutes later, dead."

"What the hell is it with Jack and Jill and you right now?" Adam asks. "Why do I think it's some sort of pre-wedding nerves that has Jill not coming down the hill?"

I ignore him and continue on, though it was a good play on words. Well done, Adam. "I don't run blind," I say. "What if I'm a target and that makes Candace a target?" My lips tighten and I do what I never do. I toss my uneaten pizza back into the box. "We're getting married in two days. We're going on our damn honeymoon."

"*We* will handle this," Blake assures me.

"Yeah, man," Adam chimes in. "Chill. Eat pizza. Have normal wedding nerves. We've got your back."

"Like I can do anything fucking normal," I say. "I'm a damn assassin getting married in a church. What the fuck is that?"

"Ex-assassin," Adam reminds me.

"Not if someone hurts Candace," I assure him. "I normally just get the job done, a quick kill, and move on. If she gets hurt, I won't be quick. I will make the responsible person suffer."

"Back to your question," Blake says. "What is normal about an *ex*-assassin marrying the love of his life in a church? Nothing, but it's good. Real damn good. What is this? Good. Real damn good. We got this. We are going to be monitoring the situation, looking for trouble. Get married. Go on your honeymoon. If you want backup when you're in California, we can make sure Candace never knows."

"I'm not going down the path of keeping secrets from Candace," I say. "And I think it would be irresponsible of me to let down my guard without backup. But let me talk to Candace."

"You want a drink, man?" Blake asks. "I've got the good stuff."

"I'd rather have a box of donuts," I say, scrubbing the back of my neck. "I need a clear head."

"That I can manage," Asher says, standing up. "We ordered this morning." He heads out of the room.

Blake's eyes meet mine. "You've changed, Rick Savage. You would never have suggested you need help in the past."

Because I didn't give a shit if I lived or died before I got Candace back, I think, but I don't say that. I know enough about Blake's past, before he met his wife, Kara, to know he knows.

"Did someone order donuts?"

At Candace's voice, the room's attention shifts to the doorway where she stands, looking like a brunette angel, holding the box of donuts. She grins at me. "I hope you don't mind me barging in on the party."

Just seeing her lights up the moment, every moment she shares with me. I still can't get over how she affects me, *every single time* I see her. I stand up and cross to meet her, taking the donuts and kissing her. "Good timing, baby." I set the donuts on the table, give Blake a look, and then turn back to Candace. "Come talk to me." I capture her hand and lead her toward a private office, and then inside, shutting the door behind us.

"Oh God," she says, turning to me. "What's wrong, Rick? What is—"

I tangle fingers in her hair, maneuver her against the wall, and say, "Not a damn thing now that you're here," I murmur, and then I kiss the hell out of her. "God, woman, you taste like the woman I have to marry."

She laughs. "And you taste like the man I have to marry." Her hand flattens on my chest. "Tell me what you need to tell me, but I read that room. There's a problem."

She misses nothing. I force myself to let her go, backing up to lean on the desk where I can study her and read her reaction better. She steps behind a chair and grabs the back. "Is it bad?"

"No," I assure her. "Not bad. In fact, Blake and Asher find no reason for us to be worried."

Her fingers curl into the cushion at the back of the chair. "What do you think?"

"I'm uneasy."

"That *word*," she says. "That's what that investor makes me feel. That's what I felt when I thought I was being watched. Uneasy."

I push off the desk and press a knee on the chair, my hands settling on her shoulders. "Our wedding will be safe. We'll have Walker handling security. But I want to go on our honeymoon and feel just as safe."

"You want to put it off? I mean, we could go to the Hamptons and look around instead? All I care about is being with you."

"She's so damn easygoing. "We're taking our honeymoon, but Blake offered us security, a chance for me to let down my guard and just be with you. We won't know they're there."

"Oh. Well, that's very generous of everyone involved. But I feel bad for them to have to just hang out while we have fun. Don't you?"

"Not bad enough to not want you to have extra protection. And I'll pay them well. So will Blake, but I'll make it extra worth their time."

"And they'll decline," she says. "You know they will."

"Maybe we can come up with a gift for each of them that they can't turn down."

Her eyes light. "I like that. Who would be coming alone? Because you know, Adam keeps talking about a Rolex."

My brows shoot up. "Adam? A Rolex?"

"The Batman Rolex. He says he can't buy it for himself. That's just silly stupid, to spend that much on a watch. But damn it's a beauty. His words, not mine."

"He has boatloads of money," I say. "Why doesn't he buy the damn watch?"

"But have you ever seen him splurge on himself?"

"No, actually, I haven't. And I don't know who will be coming, but I almost bet Adam will be on board."

"Because he's a good friend. And he needs a Batman Rolex," she jokes.

"A brother," I say. "I'd die for that man. And yes. Get him the damn Batman Rolex."

"I will, and as for dying for him. I know you would, but please don't. I worried when you were gone this time. I'm going to have to find a way to deal with the dangerous side of your life."

She worries. She's the only person who has ever worried about me. Well, maybe my mother, but she had so much to deal with my father that she had no room for much more, even me. "I already told Walker I wanted lower-risk jobs and to   stay   stateside. But I can quit. We have enough money to last a lifetime."

"No. No, I *do not* want you to quit. Saving people is what you do. It was always what you did. If you didn't have that you would be miserable. And you would not be happy just operating. We both know it. You need the high of something more."

I used to fear I'd let her down by being a soldier first and a surgeon second. I don't anymore. Especially right at this moment.

"As for our wedding," she continues, "let's go tell Blake yes on the extra security, and go home. You do have to leave tomorrow morning. Let's enjoy tonight."

I grunt at that but I don't argue. I'll deal with my objection on the topic when we're naked.

We head back to the conference room and deliver the news. "I'm in for Sonoma all the way," Adam says. "And I talked to Lucifer. He's in, too."

Lucifer being one of the new recruits, and another hacker type. "I don't know him well enough for him to be included."

"A good reason for him to do this," Adam states. "He doesn't have to be at the wedding to actually watch the wedding. As for trust. I trust him. So you trust him."

I grunt. "Okay," I say, but I'll be talking to Blake later on the topic. I grab the box of donuts. "We're out of here."

"Adam, you'll be at the house at eight in the morning?" Candace queries.

"You betcha, Candace," Adam agrees, before he stands up and looks me in the eye. "And I'm bringing Blake for reenforcements. We'll get him out of the apartment."

"I'm not leaving, asshole," I grumble.

Candace steps in front of me and wraps her arm around me. "It's bad luck to see me the day of the wedding. So no matter what, we can't be together tomorrow night. So do this for us. For luck."

"Jesus, woman," I murmur. "How am I going to say no to that?"

"You'll try," she assumes correctly. "But you'll do what's right."

Blake laughs and fuck him. I kiss Candace and get her the hell out of there before someone convinces her I need to stay away from her tonight, too.

CHAPTER TWENTY-SIX

Candace

My phone alarm goes off at seven in the morning, and I groan at the beeping noise. How can I not? I'm on my side, with Savage's big body wrapped around me, his legs tangled with mine. I don't want to get up, but suddenly my eyes pop open. "We're getting married tomorrow," I say, a lift in my voice, excitement overcoming me.

He laughs low and deep, obviously just as awake as I am, and nuzzles my neck. "Yes, we are, Candy, baby. Yes, we are. And it's only been years in the making."

"A decade," I say, rolling over to press my hand to his jaw. "A decade."

"But we wait no more," he says, and he shifts half on top of me, pressing himself against me and he clearly has more on his mind than conversation.

He leans in to kiss me. I press my hand to his mouth. "No. We cannot have sex. It's bad luck."

He grabs my hand and pulls it from his mouth, frustration in those rich blue eyes of his. "You gotta be kidding me."

"I'm not," I say quite precisely. "We shouldn't be together now." I try to scoot away.

He uses his powerful leg to hold me in place. "Oh no. I'm not done with you."

"Yes," I say. "You are."

"No," he says, widening my legs and sliding in between. "I am not."

Heat rushes through me, but my hands press firmly to his broad shoulders. "No, Rick. *No.*"

"No sex," he says. "But I do have a morning-before-our-wedding gift for you." He slides down my body and kisses my belly, his tongue dipping into my belly button, and damn him, my sex clenches.

I object. I almost sound outraged. "Sex includes all things involving the mouth."

"No man would agree with that definition at all. Ask Bill Clinton."

"No, you didn't go there."

"Oh come on. Every man has used that joke." He slides lower. "I agree with Bill. Sex is defined how I define it and the mouth doesn't count. And my opinion matters. You're marrying me." He licks my clit.

"Oh God," I breathe out. "Rick, damn it." His warm breath fans my cheek and my lashes lower and I'm beyond saying no. How can I want to say no when his tongue is now swirling around my clit, and his fingers are sliding along the sensitive seam of my body?

His mouth closes down on my clit and he suckles. My body lifts of its own accord, hips arching into him. And I'm lost. He's suckling and licking, his fingers sliding inside me, and he's just so damn good at this. He knows my body. He knows me. And there is something incredibly erotic beyond the obvious act, to having a man own you with pleasure this easily. It's a matter of a few more licks, and I am already trembling my way into release, gasping when the quake and all its intensity has passed.

His fingers slide out of me and he kisses my belly, his blue eyes brimming with heat and mischief. "A wedding gift," he repeats. "And now I'm going to take a cold shower, alone, so I don't blow your rules." He pushes off the bed and starts walking toward the bathroom.

"They aren't my rules!" I call out. "It's luck and tradition."

He just grunts and disappears into the bathroom. I sit up and twist around to sit on the edge of the bed, my body heavy and sated. His, not so much. I debate—oh, how I debate—what comes next. I should just leave him in there and follow the "rules" as he put it. But an idea comes to me. I stand up, strip off my gown and walk toward the bathroom.

Savage

I'm so damn hard I could nail something to the damn floor, but I don't have a cold shower in me right now. I turn on the water, let it warm, and step inside. I've just shut the door when it opens again and Candace steps inside, naked of course. She pushes up against me, one of her hands wrapping my cock, and presses me against the wall. "We are not having sex," she declares.

"You just wanted to hold it?" I ask, closing my hand around hers to make sure she doesn't change her mind.

"No," she says, going down on her knees.

I let go of her hand and she brings my cock to her mouth as she adds, "I just wanted to lick it."

And so, she does.

I draw in a breath and squeeze my eyes shut a moment, but not for long. I don't want to miss anything.

"Consider this a wedding gift."

133

CHAPTER TWENTY-SEVEN

Candace

Rick and I are dressed and drinking coffee when Adam and Blake arrive right on time, and with Starbucks in hand. Adam hands me my white mocha, proving he knows my favorite drink.

"God, I love my new family," I exclaim, eagerly sipping my beverage.

And while the whole group of us gather around the kitchen island, Adam smiles and offers me a small wink while Blake laughs. "Smith is picking up your friend Linda right now. She should be here at your place in forty-five minutes. And Asher is picking up your father tonight at ten. We'll let you know when we drop him at his hotel."

"Thanks, Blake," I say. "And I owe Smith and Asher."

"They don't mind," Blake says. "We're family, as you said. This is how we roll for each other."

"I still want to do something for Asher to thank you. And I hate my father is coming in so last minute anyway, but despite telling me he's retired, he had some military training event."

There's a tic in Rick's jaw and I capture his hand. "You think he's not retired at all, don't you?"

"You know what I think," Rick says. "I think he's involved in another black ops project."

"Whatever the case, and I hope that is not the case, we should have gotten you two together before the wedding just to get the past—into *the past*."

"It'll be fine," he promises me. "I love you and he loves you. We have that in common." He cups my head and kisses me. "I'm leaving before I don't leave and every minute I stand here it gets harder to walk out that door."

"And then the best man will have to kick his ass and drag him out of here," Adam says. "And I'll be obligated, since it's his wedding eve, to pretend I don't enjoy it."

"Sounds like an invitation to box a little, Navy fin boy," Rick suggests. "Let's go punch each other. It feels good."

"No," I say. "I do not want your face smashed in for the wedding, Rick."

He gives me an "are you serious?" look. "You think he's going to bust my face in?"

Adam says, "Oh fuck, now you've gone and done it."

"He's right," Rick says. "We're going to box." He eyes me. "Maybe you should come and watch."

"No," I say. "And I forbid you to go and box."

"Woman," he chides. "Who do you think you're bossing around?"

"My future husband," I remind him. "I'm the one who is sharing your life with you and who has waited years for tomorrow."

"Right," he says. "Fuck. Okay. I won't go box with Adam."

I arch a brow.

"With anyone," he concedes.

I laugh and follow the guys to the door, where Rick kisses me again and says, "See you tomorrow, Mrs. Savage."

"See you tomorrow, Mr. Savage," I reply, and he steps into the hallway where the other guys wait.

I shut the door, lean on it, and smile, a smile that I feel clear to my toes.

CHAPTER TWENTY-EIGHT

Candace

With Smith's help, Linda, Julie, and Lauren arrive at our apartment at the same time in what becomes a rush of laughter, hugs, and girl talk. And now I have an old best friend and two new ones, which turn out to be exactly what I need right now. Twins times two: two brunettes, me and Lauren, and two stunning blondes, Linda and Julie.

I show Linda to the spare bedroom for the night, and she gives me a huge hug. "I can't believe this is finally happening." She studies me. "You never stopped loving him. And you never glowed like you do right now when he was gone."

"I'm happy," I say. "And as a bonus for you, there are lots of hot men in this new family of mine. Maybe I can hook you up and one of them will lure you to New York. Adam, the best man, is single, honest, an ex-Navy SEAL, Team Six even, and good-looking. And then there is Smith." I wiggle a brow. "Cute, right?"

"Stop," she says, holding up her hands. "I'm not looking for a man. As you know, I've had my share of bad luck. And the honest, good-looking ones that aren't married are always the screwed-up ones."

"Aren't we all?" I ask.

"Yeah," she agrees. "I guess we are."

We rejoin Lauren and Julie and it's not long before we're off for a spa day at a fancy hotel. Once we're primped, waxed, massaged, and our toes and fingers have been painted, all done with Julie eating saltine crackers, we end up at a cozy table for lunch.

It's champagne for all but Julie, who orders orange juice. "When are you telling Luke?" Lauren asks, giving her a pointed look—like—*it's time.*

Julie purses her lips. "You have asked me that three times just today."

"Because I know you want the moment to be special, but you're going to a wedding tomorrow. How are you going to decline champagne when you love champagne? And do you think he doesn't know something is up?"

"Good point," Linda chimes in, already one of us and I adore her all the more for it. "What if he thinks you have some sort of unexpected regret about being pregnant?"

"See," Lauren says. "You have to tell him." She points at Linda. "And you, Linda, need to open a floral shop here and come help me defend my positions."

"Yes," I say. "Let's get her moved right here to us." I don't give Linda time to argue. I refocus on Julie. "You told me you had a plan to tell him," I remind her. "What was that again?"

"I've had several plans," she says. "We've been trying for a while, so I want this to be special. But maybe I should just tell him tonight. Actually, I think I need to go home. I need to tell him." She grabs her phone and punches a number and says, "Hey. I'm headed home. Are you there?" She listens a moment. "Great. I'll see you in a few minutes. Love you." She hangs up. "I'm going to go tell him. Oh God, why do I want to cry right now."

"Hormones," Lauren, a mother of two, assures her. "And even for a tough-as-nails mama like yourself, it's emotional and exciting." She grabs her purse. "I'm going to walk her out." She squeezes my arm. "Try to sleep. Tomorrow will be magical."

Julie rushes around the table and hugs me. "Love you, Candace. And I got the bill. I told them before we sat down."

"Thank you," I say. "And I love you, too."

And then they are gone and it's just me and Linda. "It's just us girls."

"Let's go back to your place and you can give me the full tour of that gorgeous apartment of yours," she suggests.

"Perfect," I agree, eager for some best friend time.

We gather our things and head to the lobby, where she tugs my arm. "Bathroom." She points to a sign.

I point to a couple of chairs and we split up. I spy an extra bar and I'm suddenly dying of thirst. Wasting no time making that my destination, I order a soda, which the bartender gives me on the house. I guess word got out that we spent a lot of money here today. I've just downed a big swallow when I hear, "Candace," from behind me.

At the sound of the remotely familiar male voice, I turn around to find Kirk standing there.

LISA RENEE JONES

CHAPTER TWENTY-NINE

Candace

I blink, shocked by what my eyes reveal, *who* they reveal, but it's him, it's Kirk. He's really here. And of course, he's wearing a clearly expensive blue suit. A man that I'd define as dripping money and arrogance is once again dripping money and arrogance.

"Kirk? How are you here? I thought you were leaving town?"

"You and me both," he says, unbuttoning his jacket and sliding his hands to his hips. "I had an investment go south while I was on the way to the airport. I had to turn around and come back. I'm eager to get home tomorrow. What are you doing here?"

"Pampering before the wedding," I say, eager to remind him I'm about to get married. "This is the perfect place."

"Oh right. Wedding day tomorrow." Then almost dismissively, he asks, "Can I buy you a drink to settle your nerves?"

"No thank you. I'm not much of a drinker."

That's when Linda saves the day. "Hi," she says, joining us.

Eager to shift the attention away from me, I say, "Kirk, this is my best friend, Linda. Linda, this is Kirk, the money behind a big project I'm doing."

Kirk, reluctantly it seems, glances at Linda. Linda is a beauty, worthy of anyone's attention. Yet he barely blinks at her. "Nice to meet you, Linda." He doesn't even offer her his hand. He turns back to me. "You're sure on that drink?"

I manage not to bristle. "I am," I say. "Tonight I need to go home to my soon-to-be husband." I link my arm with Linda's and add, "Right?"

"Right," she says. "He's a big bear of a man who wants his woman with him."

Oh God, what just came out of her mouth? I almost laugh and I would if I wasn't so creeped out by Kirk being here right now. "Safe travels, Kirk, and I can't wait to get started on the museum." And with that, I nudge Linda, and the two of us start walking.

"What was that about?" she whispers.

"I don't know," I say. "I just—I don't know."

"How can you not know? You were acting like he was a bee buzzing about and considering which part of you to sting."

It's an interesting analogy. That's exactly how I feel with Kirk, and I can't get in the back of the SUV Smith is driving for us tonight fast enough. Once we're inside, he glances back at us. "How was it?"

"Smith, Kirk, that investor from the museum was just in the hotel. He told me he was leaving last night and then he was here."

He twists around to face us, and he doesn't dismiss Linda. His gaze goes to her and then to me. "Did he say why?"

"I mean, it was a good explanation—last-minute business—but it feels off. I'm going to call Rick."

"I'll get you out of here and call Blake," he replies, shifting back behind the wheel and setting us in motion.

"What is going on?" Linda asks urgently.

"He just creeps me out," I say. "Didn't you feel it?"

"I felt your nervous energy around him," she replies. "He seemed interested in you, inappropriately so considering he knows you're getting married tomorrow. But nothing else."

But my gut says otherwise. I dial Rick. He answers instantly. "Miss me already?"

"I missed you the minute you walked out the door. Something weird happened."

"Tell me," he says, his tone instantly serious.

I run down the entire encounter with him. "What do you think?"

"Hold on," he says, and I can hear him talking in the background, and the low rumbles of male voices. Then there are fingers tapping on keyboards.

Rick returns to the line. "He's registered at the hotel you were at," he says. "And he's due to checkout tomorrow. Blake is going to have him monitored and make sure he really leaves and gets on a plane tomorrow."

"I won't argue against that plan," I reply, relieved by the answers he's given me. "And the fact that he's registered in the hotel is comforting." I laugh. "Maybe he thinks I'm stalking him, not the opposite."

He jumps right on that. "You think he's stalking you?"

"No," I say. "But I'd rather not see him again anytime soon."

"I'm coming home."

"You're not coming home, Rick Savage," I chide.

"This is about your safety," he argues.

"I'll stay over," Smith calls out over his shoulder, obviously overhearing what was said or just figuring out the context of our conversation.

I barely control a smile. I've caught him watching Linda. I do believe Smith would like a little more time with my best friend, and so I say, "Smith is staying the night."

Rick growls, literally growls, and says, "This rule of yours about us being apart—"

"Will make being together tomorrow all the better. Good night, love of my life."

"Candace," he pleads softly.

"Good night." I hang up and realize that was the last time I will talk to him until tomorrow when we stand before God and our guests, and he becomes my husband, and me his wife.

143

Savage

I slide my phone back into my pocket and glance between Blake and Adam, and do so over the top of several bags of burgers, a deck of cards, poker chips, and at least a half dozen empty beer bottles. "This would be a good time to talk me out of going to that hotel."

"I'm not going to talk you out of it," Blake says. "I'll go with you."

Adam throws down his cards. "I'm in."

CHAPTER THIRTY

Savage

Fifteen minutes later, I'm in the backseat of an SUV with Blake, while Asher and Adam are in the front. Asher is our driver. In the short drive to the hotel, Blake has hacked into the hotel footage, found out the room number assigned to Kirk, and then used the cameras to confirm he's presently in said room. At present, we're parked in the hotel visitor lot, eyes on the front door, and I'm watching the recorded exchange from inside the hotel between Candace and Kirk, minus sound.

"Where did he come from?" I ask when it's over.

Blake adjusts the footage, and it becomes clear that Kirk was sitting at the bar, working on a laptop, when Candace approached the bartender. Blake keys through the footage, looking for something, and then says, "He'd been there about fifteen minutes. He'd entered from the outside of the hotel, and never went to his room."

A buzzer goes off on Blake's computer. He quickly adjusts his view and we now have a visual of Kirk's room. He's just exited to the hallway.

"Where is he going, that little bastard?" I murmur.

The answer turns out to be the hotel bar again, where he proceeds to order a drink, sit down, and make a phone call. A pretty brunette sits down, orders a drink, and he seems to see an opening. The horny hound dog makes a move. And she doesn't mind. She leans all into the encounter, welcoming him to sit down with her.

"This is my cue," Adam says, glancing back at us. "By the time he convinces her to go to his room, I can be in and out."

Blake says, "Do it. Asher, go with him. We need in his computer."

"How are you going to get in the room?" I ask.

Adam gives me a "really?" look and then he and Asher exit the vehicle.

My gaze shifts back to the camera feed and to Kirk. His hand is already on the woman's leg, the bastard. "They better work fast. He sure the fuck is."

"Don't assume the worst about this," Blake cautions. "From what I'm seeing, he hit on Candace and now he's all over this chick. He could just be a horn dog."

"Spare me the comfort coddling. If you believed that bullshit, you wouldn't have two of our guys breaking into his room and stealing his computer data. Something feels off to you. Furthermore, is him being a horn dog to my future wife supposed to make me want to kill him less?" I don't wait for a reply. "Sitting here and doing nothing is making me lose my damn mind."

"Which is why I didn't fight you when you wanted to come," Blake says. "If this is nothing, you can go to your wedding tomorrow and know it's nothing."

I don't comment. I have nothing good to say. I text Candace: *Are you home?*

I am, she replies. *And my father is in his hotel room. I spoke to him about half an hour ago. When I got off, I found Smith and Linda at our island, where they remain. They're flirting. It's really adorable.*

You're adorable, I answer. *Nothing involving Smith is adorable, especially his feet. I've seen them. They're ugly.*

Because you hate feet, she accuses.

I answer with, *Not yours.*

Because you love me, she replies.

Yes, I do, I think, as Blake points to the camera footage and I quickly understand what he's telling me. The woman is holding her room key out to Kirk. He accepts it and they both stand.

"Thank fuck, they're going to her room," Blake murmurs.

And thank fuck turns out to be real damn right, considering it's another fifteen minutes before Adam climbs back into the vehicle. He's wearing a staff uniform. We don't ask where he got it. "No weapons," Adam announces.

"I did a surface check of his computer," Asher adds. "Checked his socials and email. He looks clean. There were a shit ton of business documents for his company, but nothing that looked off." He holds up a drive. "I got everything he had. I'll spend a couple of hours tonight doing a deeper check"

Blake's phone buzzes with a text. He glances at it and then says, "Let's get out of here. Lucifer and Dexter are now on the premises and going nowhere. They're going to discreetly see Kirk through security at the airport tomorrow morning."

I draw in a breath and Adam rotates around in his seat to look at me. "It's time to think about you and Candace, man. You're marrying her tomorrow. Live in the moment with her."

He's right. He's absolutely fucking right.

I motion for Asher to take us home.

Live in the moment.

I'm all in.

But I want a whole lot more than a moment with Candace.

And I can't seem to agree with the idea that Kirk's only sin is to be a horny bastard.

It doesn't feel right.

CHAPTER THIRTY-ONE

Candace

Nerves get the best of me. I can't sleep. I know I can't sleep.

"We have to go to bed," Linda presses for the third time, laying on Rick's side of the bed, both of us in long john style pajamas.

Apparently, she's not as obsessed with Fixer Upper as I am, because she says, "I have spoken," grabs the remote and turns off the tv. "You need your beauty sleep," she explains.

"I *can't* sleep," I repeat for about the fourth time. I change the subject. "You're sure you and Smith weren't flirting?"

"I'm not looking for a man," she says, avoiding a direct answer. "I came prepared for you tonight." She reaches into a little bag she has beside the bed and produces NyQuil and melatonin. "It's a magical combination."

I allow her to drug me and then she says, "I'm going to my room, but I'm taking the remote. Your obsession with Fixer Upper is out of control."

She's not joking. She grabs her bag and the remote, walks to the door, turns out the light, and leaves. I sigh, check my alarm and lay my phone on my stomach, certain I will be surfing the web any minute to keep from going crazy in the dark. Still, I shut my eyes, and silly as it sounds, I start counting sheep.

Savage

I'm up at five AM with Adam, in his gym working out, running a good five miles on the treadmill before a hard lift. After, Adam makes coffee, egg whites, and bacon. I spend the time he's cooking scouring through all the research Asher and Blake did on Kirk, Max, and anyone else connected to my past. It all seems to come together on the right side of things.

Adam refills my coffee cup. "Let it go. Me and Lucifer will be along for every second of the next ten days. And Lucifer is a wicked good hacker. He's a good add-on to this trip. Trust me. Just go get married." He pours a crapload of creamer in my coffee.

I grab the cup and take a sip. It's good. And today will be good.

"I'm getting married," I say. "She said yes."

He grins. "Yes. She did." He laughs. "I still remember when she saw you for the first time in years. You got into a bar fight next door to Linda's floral shop."

"Because she told me Candace was engaged to another man."

"And then Candace showed up and you told her you wanted to kiss her. To which she slapped you. I should have known she still loved you right then."

I grin. "That did kind of give it away, didn't it?"

"When she still feels so much that she has to slap you, that's the next best thing to a kiss," he agrees. "Go shower, you stinky bastard. It's time to go make this last forever." He shuts the MacBook in front of me and I let him.

It's time to make this all about me and Candace. And only all about me and Candace.

Candace

Suddenly, I'm blinking awake to the sound of my alarm and gasping to realize I fell asleep. And now, it's my wedding day. It's here. Today is the day I marry Rick Savage. I glance at my phone and it's almost ten, which was the plan. I wanted to sleep late and look good today. But now it's really today, *the day*. I sit up, and I'm so overwhelmed with emotions that I don't know if I want to laugh or cry. There's a knock on the door, and Linda pokes her head in. "I brought coffee."

"You're a goddess," I say. "First you drug me and now you bring me coffee."

She grins and crosses to join me, her blonde hair sticking up all over the place. Maybe she isn't flirting with Smith. I sip from the cup. "You ah—let Smith see you like that?"

"He did," she says. "And he laughed. And I don't care that he's a hot guy who saw me look like shit. I don't want him to want me. I don't want to want him."

"I see," I say, grinning and sipping my coffee. "But you do, don't you?"

"No," she snips. "No. No. No." She glances at the clock and changes the subject. "It's ten. The wedding is at two. You'll have a light lunch catered in here at eleven, then we leave for the church, where the stylist will meet you. There will be a one o'clock snack to ensure you don't fall on your face walking down the aisle. Do you want to shower before or after lunch?"

"After. And you have it all under control, don't you?"

"What's a maid of honor for if not to take care of the bride? Especially since you declined a bachelorette party. What do you need or want to do before the food arrives?"

"Where's the remote?"

She reaches in her pocket and sets it on the bed. I grab it and turn on Fixer Upper. She rolls her eyes. "Are you serious?"

"It calms my nerves, and besides, Rick and I are going to buy a house in the Hamptons. I love seeing the inspiration for décor."

"Oh, the Hamptons. Fancy, my queen." She bows and laughs. "I'm going to get coffee and then I'll watch with you."

I smile and my cellphone buzzes with a message. I grab it from beside me where it's fallen to find a message from Rick: *Finally. Today.*

My heart squeezes and I reply back with, *Finally. Today.*

CHAPTER THIRTY-TWO

Candace

It's one-twenty, forty minutes before I'm to become Mrs. Rick Savage.

At present, I'm in a pink robe, standing in the dressing room in the section of the church used for wedding preparation, staring into a three-way mirror. My hair is glossy and around my shoulders. My makeup is pale pink perfect. Both thanks to the stylist, Jessica.

"Are you pleased?" Jessica queries eagerly, shoving long locks of curly red hair behind her ears, waiting anxiously for my reply.

I don't know how she can be anxious at all. She's brilliant, a true artist and suddenly, I am emotional, so very emotional, and I think I might cry.

"You did a perfect job," I say, my voice a rasp, my eyes burning. "I love it."

"Yay!" she says, clapping her hands. "I'm so pleased, but my job was easy. You're gorgeous. We'll get you in your dress and your veil in," she glances at her watch, "in about fifteen minutes. I don't want you to have time to step on it. And you can't sit once you put it on."

"I think I'll sit now, actually," I say, making my way to the vanity chair and I ease to the cushion, grateful as it absorbs my unsteady weight.

There's a knock on the door and Linda peeks her head in. "You nervous?"

"So bad," I admit and I hold out my hand. "I'm trembling."

153

LISA RENEE JONES

"That's natural," she assures me as she steps into the room, looking gorgeous in a silver floor-length, figure-hugging gown. Each of my girls are wearing different colors. I wanted them to pick something they'd wear again and love forever.

"Everything is going as planned," Linda says, shutting the door. "Adam has the rings. I made sure he has yours. And I brought champagne to calm your nerves."

Seeing her dress fully now, I give her dress choice a critical inspection. The conclusion is perfection. "You look beautiful," I proclaim and motion to her updo. "Your hair is amazing."

"Jessica's sister did it," she says. "I love her." She eyes Jessica. "And you, too." She offers her one of the two glasses in her hand. "For you."

Jessica waves her off. "I'd better not. I need to take care of Candace now and through her change of clothes."

"Understood," Linda says, "and that proves why I love you and your sister. You're professionals." She offers me the glass.

I try to wave it off. "Oh no," I say. "I can't be drunk for my wedding. Rick will think I needed to be drunk to go through with it. He's always afraid I'll decide I'm marrying a monster."

"Drink," she orders. "I know you don't handle it well, but next to a Xanax that would knock you out, this is the next best thing. You can't walk steadily if you're shaking."

She's right. And I'm a wreck. I accept the glass and sip. "How *is* Rick?"

"Pacing his room, so I hear." She sips the champagne and sets her glass on the vanity. "He sent you your 'something new' to wear."

I blink. "He did?"

"He said he knew you were fretting about something new, something borrowed, and something blue, so he thought he'd cover two for one for you." She pulls up a chair and sits beside me, slipping the small silver bag hanging at her shoulder around to her lap, as she reaches inside.

A moment later, she produces a velvet bag. "It came in a box and bag, but I took it out of the box because I didn't have enough hands to carry it," she explains, offering it to me. Anxiously, I open the bag to find a thin silver bracelet with delicate little turquoise hearts dangling from the strand.

"It's beautiful!" Linda and Jessica exclaim at the same time.

"It is beautiful," I whisper and I give a little laugh. "I have a blue button I borrowed from Jessica pinned to my garter, and I decided my dress was new, so it counted as the something new."

"Well you were wrong but he made it beautifully right." Linda and Jessica say at the same time, only to laugh at the shared moment.

I try to put on the bracelet, but my hands are trembling too much to get it done. Linda orders me to drink, and then finishes the job for me. "And you can give back the button," she says when the bracelet is secure. "I have your something old and borrowed." She's back to digging in the silver bag and she pulls out a mesh black bag this time.

"Surprise," she says. "That's special."

Curious now, I open the bag and my heart squeezes with what I find. "My mother's cross that she kept on her at all times." My gaze jerks to hers. "How did you get that?"

"Your father gave it to me. He's waiting to see you, but he knew you wouldn't be dressed. He wanted you to place it wherever you wanted to place it in privacy."

I start to tear up and her and Jessica both say, "Do not cry!"

"You'll mess up your makeup," Jessica warns.

"I know," I say, and I down half the glass of champagne. "I'm going to cry."

"Don't," Linda orders. "Wait until later. As your father always says, mind over matter. I was thinking you could pin the cross to your garter."

"Perfect," I say, parting my robe to attach the cross. I met Rick right after losing my mother. He helped me survive her loss. Emotion pinches in my chest. I loved her so much. I thought she'd be here the day I got married. I let my dress fall back into place and murmur. "It's perfect."

"It's time to get dressed," Jessica announces.

"I need to see my father," I object.

"Once you're dressed," Jessica insists. "Down that champagne, go pee—it will be hard in the dress—and then let's get you dressed."

"I'll let him know you're dressing and keep him busy," Linda promises, heading for the door. "And I'll get him away from the door so you can go pee without interruption."

And then she's gone.

I let out a breath. I'm putting on my dress. This is really happening.

CHAPTER THIRTY-THREE

Savage

I'm in my tuxedo, sans the jacket, nervous energy exploding from every part of me, my feet leading me back and forth across the dressing room. "Stop pacing," Adam orders. "And drink this."

He hands me a glass of whiskey and I wave him off. "I can't drink. She'll think I needed liquid courage to say I do. She believes I'll back out to save her from a life with me."

"Or that you're nervous as fuck and needed to calm the hell down to remember your vows. Drink."

I down the whiskey and hand him the glass. "Do you have the rings?" I stop walking and face him, patting my pockets. "Shit. The rings—"

"I have the rings."

I breathe out. "Thank fuck. And we're sure Linda gave her the bracelet?"

"I just gave it to her fifteen minutes ago and she was headed to see Candace."

"Right. Right." I draw in a breath and then, "Did Adrian make it in?" I ask. Adrian Mack is one of my groomsmen, and he's been in Germany on a job for Walker, arriving back just in time for the wedding. It's him, Adam, and Blake standing up with me.

"He's here and changing into his tux now."

This is good news. I wanted him here, but the job he was on got nasty, and for a moment there, I wasn't sure he could make it. Adrian and I might not be as tight as I am with Adam and Blake, but he was with me when I won Candace back. He helped me save her life.

There's a knock on the door, and Blake pokes his head in. "Thirty-minute warning." He steps inside, already spiffy in his tuxedo. "The church is full. The decorations are beautiful. All is well." He gives me a keen inspection. "How are you feeling, man?"

"Like my head's going to explode."

"I remember that very feeling," he assures me. "You'll settle down the minute you see her. I promise."

"Thank you for making this church happen, Blake. She gets to be a princess today. She deserves that after the shit I put her through."

"You both deserve it," he says. "I hope you figure that out right about now, considering you're at your own wedding."

There's another knock on the door and Adrian enters. "I'm here, man. I made it." He tugs on his lapels. "Latin man in a tuxedo, freshly trimmed goatee, and ravishing personality. The wedding can go on."

"He's losing his shit," Blake says. "Why don't you tell him a joke? I know he loves your jokes." He eyes me. "I'll be ready when you are." He exits the room.

"Me, too," Adam says. "I need to go see how we're looking out there."

"Fuck, don't leave me alone with Adrian and his bad jokes."

Too late. He does just that.

"All right," Adrian says. "A ghost walks into a bar—"

I groan.

He starts again, "A ghost walks into a bar, and the bartender says, 'Sorry, we don't serve spirits.' Give it a minute. It will sink in. You know because spirits—"

"I get it," I say. "Stop talking."

There's another knock on the door. Adrian walks in that direction and opens it. The next thing I know, he's disappearing, and fuck me, Candace's dad is stepping into the room. Damn Adrian for not warning me. "General," I greet.

"Son," he says, shutting the door. "I just wanted a moment with you."

"You going to try to send me off on some assignment to save the world and destroy your daughter?"

His lips press together. "I had good intentions when I recruited you, Savage. A surgeon and soldier with skills like yours doesn't exist. Except you. You are one of a kind. The kind of man I thought could save lives."

"You made me a killer."

"As long as I was involved, every kill you made saved lives," he insists.

"You wanted me out of Candace's life."

"You're a strange combination, Savage. A man who can save a life and take a life. I admit I wasn't keen on you with my daughter. But I was wrong. If Candace's mother was alive, she would have long ago beaten my ass over you, Rick Savage. Ironically, you helped Candace survive her loss."

"I wish I could have met her, sir. I've heard many stories."

"She would have told me that a man like you would kill and die for the woman he loves. And you love my daughter. And she loves you."

"I do love her. More than you can possibly know."

"Then marry her and take good care of her. And maybe, just maybe, one day we can put the past behind us, and be father and son." He pauses. "Speaking of. Is your father attending today?"

Now my lips press together. "I didn't invite him."

"I see," he says, and I believe he does. I know Candace has told him about my father's abuse of my mother, as well as her miserable life before she died. I also know the general checked me out before inviting me onto his special ops team, and probably sooner because I was seeing his daughter, and did so with enough depth to know everything there is to know about me. "That's rough," he comments solemnly. "I'm here. One day, as I said, maybe that will matter to you. I'll see you at the front of the church." He starts to turn and hesitates. "For what it's worth, which is likely not much, you have my blessing."

The words punch me in the chest. He's reaching for the door and I feel a compulsion that has me saying, "It matters.

You're her father. She loves you. And for that reason alone, I'd protect you with my life." And then, because I've seen a few behavior patterns through his communication with Candace, that doesn't sit right, I add, "But don't do something stupid and repeat history. Don't try for a do-over with a new task force. We did it. It went badly. It's over."

He glances back at me over his shoulder and says, "I'll keep that in mind."

And then he opens the door and disappears into the hallway.

Adam and Adrian step back into the room.

It's almost time.

CHAPTER THIRTY-FOUR

Candace

I'm standing in front of the mirror again. And my dress is stunning, the flowers on the skirt and veil even more beautiful today than I remembered in the store.

"The veil." Linda sighs. "It's sweeping all the way down to the floor and beyond. It's just breathtaking."

There's a knock on the door. "I'm guessing that will be your father," Linda says, glancing at Jessica. "Let's give them a moment alone."

The door opens and it's Julie, looking stunning in a pale pink gown. "Your father is waiting to see you, but I just wanted to wish you luck. Lauren is helping at the door or she'd be here, too. And oh my God, you're beautiful. Savage is going to lose his mind when he sees you."

"Thank you," I say, and needing something other than the many guests about to watch me potentially trip down the aisle, I ask, "Me aside for a moment, did you tell Luke about the baby?"

"I did." She smiles. "And he's already being a protective papa bear. He's funny but so very happy. It's wonderful."

Linda, Jessica, and I ask her questions for a few minutes but Jessica returns us all to the moment, and me. "Me and my sister will help you get to where you're going without damaging your gown."

There's another knock on the door. My eyes go wide. "Is it time?"

"Not yet," Julie assures me. "You're fine on time."

Julie opens the door and then points at Linda and Jessica to follow her. I frown, confused, as they all wordlessly disappear into the hallway.

That's when my father steps into the room. Of course, that's why they left.

"There she is!" he exclaims, shutting the door and looking debonair in his tuxedo, his gray hair neatly groomed, his newly grown goatee rather handsome on him. "My God," he gushes. "You're beautiful. Your mother should be here. Damn it, I'm going to cry. Grown men don't cry."

"Yes, she should be. And now, you're going to make me cry and mess up my makeup."

"Oh no, honey. Don't you dare cry," he commands in his best general voice.

I laugh and sober quickly. "I need you to be happy for me. I love him with all my heart."

"And he loves you. I know. I just saw him. We had a chat."

"And?"

"And I believe that man would die and come back from the grave and do it again to protect you and keep you happy. I made mistakes, honey. I regret those mistakes. I didn't want you to end up with a guy like me."

"Funny. I wanted a guy just like you."

"I think you did better," he says, and my heart swells with his approval.

The door opens and Linda announces, "*Now*, it's time."

My heart flutters and butterflies explode in my belly. "Oh gosh. Oh gosh. What if I fall, Dad? What if I trip and fall in front of all of those people?"

"Then I'm quite sure Savage will pick you up and carry you to the front of the church."

"Rick," I say. "Today, he's my Rick."

"Rick," he amends.

Jessica rushes into the room and offers me my bouquet of lilacs and lilies. They were my mother's favorite flowers and that's why they decorated the entire church. I wanted her with me, with us.

"Rick," Linda announces, "is already at the front of the church. And he looks handsome."

Tears burn my eyes and I fight them hard. In a rush of activity, I'm at the entrance to the chapel, and the wedding march music starts. My father offers me his arm. "Ready, princess?"

"Since the moment I met him," I whisper, accepting his arm and seeking out Rick, who is so far away right now, too far away.

We start walking down the center of the room, and the seats are filled with people. Military friends of my family and his. Doctors from the hospital in San Antonio where Rick started his career. Clients of Walker Security who became Rick's friends, many of whom are alive today because of him. I don't know how he can call himself a monster. One day I'll make him see the truth in himself is much grander.

Finally, I can see the front of the room, where all three of my ladies, and friends, are lined up in a rainbow of silver, pink, and cream, just opposite Rick's handsome best man and groomsmen. But my focus is on Rick, and the closer I get to him, the calmer I become. But that moment, that moment, where he steps to the center of the aisle to greet me, and our eyes meet, it undoes me in ways I've never been undone. My father goes to hand me off and Rick catches me to him and kisses me. The room hums with voices and I laugh. "You weren't supposed to do that yet."

"I couldn't help myself," he assures me. "You look beautiful, baby."

"You don't look so shabby yourself," I whisper. "I can't believe we're finally doing this."

"Oh, we are," he says, his fingers brushing my cheek. "And I'm a lucky man. I want to make this official before you change your mind."

"Never, and yes, now."

And so, we step in front of the priest and the ceremony begins. And when it comes time for our vows, after much debate, Rick and I decided to say only a few short sentences each. Enough to get the point across to each other without the world knowing our private thoughts. The priest explains this to the crowd. Rick goes first. "There's a song called *Love You Like I Used To*. I don't love you like I used to, Candace. I love you more than every single day before."

Now I tear up because those few words speak so much to our lives we've shared together and apart. Now it's my turn and I say, "You're a good man, Rick Savage. I know it. Everyone in this church knows it. It is my vow that one day you will know it, too. You make me whole. I need you. Don't you dare forget that." And now I'm crying.

Rick kisses me again, and the crowd goes nuts. The priest clears his throat. "Not yet."

Rick and I laugh, as does everyone else, as he says, "The rings please."

Eagerly, impatiently, Rick and I exchange rings, and then it's time to say I do.

"Do you, Rick Savage, take Candace Marks as your lawfully wedded wife?"

"I do," he says. "With every fiber of my being."

I smile as the question is reversed. "Do you, Candace Marks, take Rick Savage to be your lawfully wedded husband?"

"I do," I say. "With every fiber of my being."

The priest has barely said the words, "I now pronounce you man and wife," before Rick is kissing me again, and it's a toe-curling, intense kiss. I'm pretty sure we leave the entire room breathless, even the priest. And when it's done, Rick whispers in my ear, "I love you, Candace Savage."

"I love you, too, Rick Savage."

Now, Rick is smiling as the priest turns us toward the crowd, and what a crowd it is. Luke is watching Julie from the front row. Lauren is between her husband, Royce, the eldest Walker, and Kara. Asher and his wife, Sierra, are there. I even find Smith and Lucifer, too. I see so many faces of those I now call family. The priest proudly announces, "I now introduce you to Mr. and Mrs. Savage."

The room erupts in applause, whispers, and claps. And together, hand in hand, Rick and I walk down the center row toward the doors of the church, married. And it only took us what feels like a lifetime. But what matters is that we still have a lifetime before us.

LISA RENEE JONES

CHAPTER THIRTY-FIVE

Candace

I change into a chic, shorter version of my dress for the reception with a few sexy surprises underneath for Rick later.

This portion of our special day is held in a gorgeous building adjacent to the church, complete with a covered and heated courtyard, decorated with the same lilacs in my bouquet. And appropriately, it seems, that is where I throw my bouquet. To my delight, Linda catches it, but then she panics and hands it to Jessica.

Rick and I are laughing as we head back inside and to the front of the room where the cakes await us. One is a towering white coconut cream with all white flowers because Rick insisted that I'm "pure as snow." Silly man. And his is all chocolate because he's a "dark as fuck bastard." His words, not mine. Whatever the case, they turned out beautiful and as a room full of people sitting at cute little tables watches us, we cut the cakes, laughing as we feed each other bites.

When it's time for the first dance, Rick has them play the song he'd referenced from our vows, *Love You Like I Used To*, and it's magical. Everything about the night is magical.

Rick and I dance, we sing, we pose for photos, and we laugh, we laugh so much.

Hours later, we depart the reception and climb into a limousine that drives us home. We'll leave on our five-hour honeymoon flight tomorrow. Tonight is for us.

We arrive at our apartment and I swear I'm as nervous as the first night I met Rick. Which is ridiculous. He's my husband now. We walk through the lobby hand in hand and the doorman waves and congratulates us on our new union. Once we're in the elevator, Rick knows just how to get me over my nerves. He presses me against the wall and his fingers dive into my hair. "Mine," he says softly. "*Wife.*"

Just that easily, my nipples are puckered, my sex clenching.

I slide my arms under his jacket and say, "Mine. *Husband.*"

"Now you can do anything you want to me," he teases.

I laugh. "But I couldn't before?"

"Good point, but now it's legal."

I laugh again and he kisses me before he whispers, "You said I do."

I smile. "So did you," and the minute his mouth comes back down on mine, the elevator doors open.

He steals a quick taste and then captures my hand. "Let's go home, wifey."

He leads me out of the elevator and to our door. He unlocks it, kicks it open, and scoops me up. I'm laughing again as he carries me across the threshold, but once inside he sets me down to lock up. I frown, surprised he's doing that right now when we have other things on our minds. Not that he doesn't usually lock up, but my gut says he's still on edge, still worried about trouble. I mean, of course, he is. We have a chaperoned honeymoon.

The apartment now secure, Rick catches my hand and walks me to him, our legs pressed together, the locked door forgotten. And for a moment we just stand there, staring at each other, this crazy mix of heat and emotion burning between us. He moves first, his hand gently cupping my face, the touch, that one touch, managing to lift goosebumps on my skin. That's how much this man affects me. He leans in, his breath warm, filled with the promise of so many things before his lips caress my lips, so tender, so slow, and I swear I feel him in every part of my body inside and out.

His fingers splay at my hip, and then his mouth slants over mine, and with that connection, it's as if the passion just explodes between us. We're kissing and touching, and he's shrugging out of his jacket and I'm pressed against the wall, his big wonderful body crowding mine. The skirt to my dress ends up at my waist. His palm is on my bare backside, a hot branding that only makes me say, oh yes, God yes. I want more. And that's what I get. In a blur of heat and desire, the dress is unzipped down the front, and his hand is on my now bare breast, the lingerie I wore for him pushed aside.

"Wait," I manage with that realization, my hand pressing on his chest. "I have lingerie on for you."

"We're just getting started, baby," he says. "You can model it for me later."

His fingers curve under my leg, just reaching my sex, and I gasp, but I grab his arm.

"I really want you to see the lingerie."

He pulls back to study me a moment, and I say, "What?"

"You really want to show me?" he asks.

"Is that bad?"

"No, baby." His lips curve. "It's fucking perfect. You're fucking perfect and I just need to slow down. Not an easy thing to do when you just became Mrs. Savage."

My lips curve now. "I love how that sounds."

"Good, because that's your new name and it's not changing again." He kisses me, hard and fast, and then pulls the skirt of my dress down.

I yelp as he surprises me, scooping me up, and starts walking.

LISA RENEE JONES

CHAPTER THIRTY-SIX

Candace

Rick might have reined in the heat momentarily, but he doesn't even try and make it to the bedroom.

He carries me toward the living room, where he sets me in front of the couch and moves the coffee table, already pulling his button-down over his head and tossing it away. "Show me," he orders gently.

I grab his waistband and say, "You first."

He arches a brow. "You want me naked first?"

"For once," I say firmly. "Yes. You first."

His eyes dance with mischief and he toes off his shoes. "What the wifey wants, the wifey gets." He strips down and stands there naked, his thick cock jutted forward, his lean muscular body a magnificent, powerful sight. He's gorgeous. And he's mine.

"Now what?" he asks, holding his hands out to his sides.

I wet my dry lips. "Sit," I order, pointing at the couch.

"Yes, ma'am," he says, and so he does.

I laugh, a little high on this power of mine that won't last. He likes control. I like him in control. But this is fun. I give him my back, fix my bra, and finish unzipping the front of my dress, which was designed to run top to bottom. Once it's hanging open, my pretty strappy white bra is exposed, and quite uplifting in all the right ways. My lacy bridal white garter belt wraps my waist and holds up white lace-top stockings. As for my panties, well—they're barely there. I drop the dress and Rick gives a little moan of approval. This has me smiling and feeling oddly shy. He's so intensely male and while turning him on is arousing and empowering, it's a bit intimidating at times. I cover myself with my hands and turn around.

His eyes sweep over me and lift to my face. "Why are you covering yourself, baby?"

Heat rushes to my cheeks and I confess, "I don't know," in a low whisper.

He stands up and closes the space between us, easing my hands from my breasts and kissing my ring finger. Warmth spreads through my body and the shyness begins to fade. I have no idea why that little act, him kissing my ring is so erotic, but it is, incredibly so, in fact. He gives me a slow inspection and then his hands cup my neck under my hair, an intimate, dominant touch, that has my sex clenching.

He tilts my gaze to his and says, "You are stunning. So fucking beautiful. And for so many reasons, Candace, I don't know how I lived without you. I don't want to try again." His voice is not about sex. It's pure, raw, emotion. Oh yes, the shyness is gone. This is me and Rick. This is us and we are as right as anything ever could be in my life.

He kisses me, another gentle caress of lips to lips, before he deepens the connection with a long stroke of his seductive tongue.

I moan with the taste of possessiveness on his tongue and soon we end up on the couch, with me straddling him, and unhooking my bra, and tossing it aside. I don't need it anymore. He saw it. Now he sees me. His cock is in front of me and I stroke it. He groans and drags my mouth to his, licking past my teeth, his fingers rolling my nipples.

"Take off the panties," he orders roughly. "I need inside you now."

"They have a slit," I whisper, and that's all he needs to hear. He captures my waist and lifts me, pressing inside me, anchoring me as I slowly slide down him until he's buried inside me.

And then, all that shyness is gone. There is nothing but passion and the man I love. I rock with him, and the heat between us is scorching. The passion is so intense I barely recognize the sounds I'm making, but there is just such a deep ache in me for this man, I cannot do anything but try to sate it. He must feel the same, the need for more, because he rolls me over and captures my mouth and one of my legs, and then drives into me. *Yes. Yes, that's it,* I want to say, but I can't speak. He thrusts again and again, and I am suddenly there, in that sweet place I both resist and crave, so very badly. I'm trembling and he groans, a deep guttural groan, his head tilted back, his face contorted in pleasure, and then he's shuddering into release. I'm done just enough before him to enjoy the display of all that power he possesses in complete abandon.

And then we melt into each other and the couch, Rick sliding to the side just enough to protect me from his weight. For long moments, we lay like that until I say, "You liked the lingerie?"

He laughs low and deep and leans on his elbow to look at me. "I loved you in the lingerie."

"And the cake? It was good, right? Especially yours. They liked the half you didn't eat."

He chuckles. "Yes. They did seem to like the half I didn't eat." He eases to my side fully and rolls me to face him. "It was perfect." His hands slide down my leg and over the cross pinned to my stocking.

He glances toward it and I explain, "My mother's cross. My father gave it to me."

His eyes warm. "Like I said. It was perfect. She was there with you."

"She was," I say. "She would have loved it. And you." I rest my hands on his face. "I can't believe we did it. We're here. We did this. We're married."

"Yes, we did this," he says, stroking hair from my face. "And now it's just you and me against the world."

"I like that. Just you and me against the world."

"Forever," he says.

"Forever."

CHAPTER THIRTY-SEVEN

Savage

Candace doesn't just roll with the punches when it comes to having escorts on our honeymoon. She brings them breakfast. We step on the private Walker-owned jet just in time for an eight AM flight to San Francisco set to last a good five hours. We're greeted by Adam and Lucifer, who are already on board, in the front of the plane. "Morning, Fin Boy," I greet Adam, and to Lucifer, "Morning, devil boy."

Candace, on the other hand, hands them each a bag so full they both have half of McDonald's menu inside. "The breakfast of champions," she says. "Thank you for doing this. You're amazing."

The guys are all blown up with big heads that I'll have to smash down later. And I get the chance when they start playing poker, and Candace is so unfazed by their presence that she suggests we play. My little wifey proceeds to beat all our asses.

"Army brat," she declares. "If you can't play poker, you're a disgrace among the ranks."

About halfway through the play, I don't miss the way she digs for the perfect gift for Lucifer, either. "Where are you from?"

"Austin, Texas."

"Oh wow," she says. "We're from San Antonio. Adrian is from Texas, too. Is your family still there?"

"They're dead," he states, tossing in his cards. "And you're killing me."

I also don't miss the way he tries to move away from the topic of his parents.

"Were they military?" she asks, because Candace isn't one to be put off.

"My father was. My mother owned a couple of coffee shops. She smelled like coffee beans all the damn time."

Adam tosses in his cards. "You won again, Candace. If Savage wasn't your husband now, I'd call you a bitch."

"And I'd bitch slap you," I assure him.

"No, you wouldn't," Candace replies, "Because I can take it like a soldier. I am a bitch. The one that just beat you again, Adam."

We all laugh. We never get back to Lucifer's story, but for the first time, I see him as more than the guy I don't really know or trust. I still don't trust him, but I'm not hating him either.

"I need a nap," I say, catching Candace's hand. "And I know you need a nap."

Her cheeks flush at my reference to last night, which included very little sleep. "Ah, yes. A nap would be good." She stands up and together we head to the rear of the plane, where I pull the curtain. There's actually a fold-out bed, and despite my best efforts otherwise, all we use it for is sleep. The good news, if there is any good news, to being in bed with Candace and only sleeping, is that we arrive with a hell of a time change and we don't feel like shit.

That night we stay in San Francisco, walk down to the docks, and spend time at a little restaurant with a view. The next morning, we head to Sonoma and Candace is like a little kid, she's so excited. "I have always wanted to go to wine country," she says as we load in the rental, driving separately from the guys. I'm making every effort, and so are they, to make this trip about me and Candace and to downplay how present our protection has to stay.

On the way to Sonoma, Candace lures me into a "how well do you know me" game.

"What's my favorite food?"

"You act like I just met you. Macaroni and cheese. What's mine?"

"A hamburger, but donuts are a close second. What's my favorite movie?" she asks.

"An Officer and a Gentleman because you're a sap. What's mine?"

"You tell everyone it's Blade with Wesley Snipes because you're not a sap. In truth, it's The Wrestler and it makes you cry every time when it shouldn't make you cry."

"He loses everything, baby. He's washed up." I ball my fist at my chest. "That shit gets real."

She laughs, and it's such a damn perfect delicate little laugh. A little goofy and somehow, I like it all the more.

We arrive in Sonoma at the swanky hotel, where I've opted for a suite with a balcony and view of rolling mountains and green fields over a private mansion, for safety reasons. Adam and Lucifer will be next door. Once our luggage arrives, I tip the bellman and do what any respectable newlywed would do. I get Candace naked.

She's standing on the balcony. I come up behind her and nuzzle her neck. "I want you," I say. "Right here."

"Here? As in on the balcony?"

"That's right."

She whirls around, her skirt lifting in the breeze. "We can't do it on the balcony."

I catch that floaty skirt and proceed to prove her wrong. It's not long before I'm inside her, and she's forgotten where we are. As it should be on our honeymoon. And if I keep her in the room naked, who needs Adam and Lucifer?

However, the minute we're dressed, she says, "Let's go downtown. I heard it's adorable."

I almost laugh at the contrasting version of myself. The man who used to kill people for a living and the man who goes to see what the adorable downtown of Sonoma looks like. But that is exactly what I'm about to do and enjoy every fucking minute.

I text Adam: *We're going to the adorable downtown.*

He replies with: *Actually, it's pretty adorable. I've seen it.*

I laugh and Candace's brows furrow in question. I show her the message exchange and now she laughs. "I kind of love that I can make you both say adorable."

She links her arm with mine and to the door we go. And I'm smiling all the way to the hired car and beyond. We leave the car behind at the center of town and begin strolling the "adorable" town, walking in and out of little stores, just enjoying life together. It's not until we're sitting at a little bar, drinking wine, that I become uneasy. And uneasy for me means trouble. The kind that makes me kill someone. And that is not what a man wants to feel on his honeymoon, not even me.

CHAPTER THIRTY-EIGHT

Savage

I text Adam: *My radar is going off. Tell me I'm being paranoid.*

We have eyes on you and all looks good, he replies. *But we'll stay alert.*

Candace's hand slides to my leg and she draws me back to her. Slowly, I ease out of that paranoia and live fully in the moment. Soon me and my baby are drinking another glass of wine and I'm back to enjoying myself despite a nagging sense of something being off. It doesn't disappear, it just fades, and I let it do so because Adam and Lucifer are nearby. Because I know that I love this woman, and I want to protect her to such a degree that I could see danger in an ant right about now.

When Candace and I finally decide to leave our cozy little spot, we do so reluctantly, and with a vow to return before we leave. "At least once before we leave," Candace insists.

"You assume you won't find a few other places you like just as much," I remind her. "But at least once," I agree.

Pleased with my answer, she moves on. "You know," she says, as I pay the bill, "before we call the car, I saw ice cream down the road. You want to get ice cream?"

"Is that a real question?" I ask. "I scream for ice cream. You scream for me."

Her cheeks flush and she nudges me. "You're so bad."

"And you love it."

"And you. I love you," she says.

Sometimes when she says those things to me, so damn easily, I wonder how a bastard like me got one chance with

179

a woman like her, let alone two. Sometimes I think she just pretends I was never who, and what, I was. And sometimes I think that one day she'll wake up and remember. And it will not be in my favor.

We head for the exit, her arm linked with mine, and she smiles up at me. And then almost as if she's read my mind, she assures me she knows exactly who, and what, I was, and still am. "Rick Savage," she says, "ex-assassin, turned domestic, on his way to get ice cream with his wife. I'm pretty sure there are a lot of people who won't believe it."

"Well, fuck those people. If I want to stroll in an adorable town and eat gobs of ice cream with my wife, I will." And because I've learned that despite my fear of losing her, I have to be me, or this will never work, I add, "And I can still kill anyone who needs killing."

"Yes, you can," she says, and as we exit to the street she halts and turns to face me and adds, "And believe it or not, Rick Savage, I find that incredibly sexy."

I pull her to me. "You shouldn't, but I'm glad you do."

Heat burns between us, but the door to the restaurant opens and explodes with people. We step right and when she shivers from the swift shift from the sixties to the evening forty-something mountain air, I quickly grab the light jacket she's holding, and help her put it on. Then I slide my arm around her and set us in motion.

Adam

Lucifer and I are perched on the low rooftop of a building, him sitting on the ground with his MacBook open, me with binoculars, watching Candace and Rick stroll downtown Sonoma.

"Dexter just got here," Lucifer informs me. "He's grabbing us food."

"My stomach says thank you, but tell me again, why the hell is he here?"

"He said and I quote: 'Why the hell did I think visiting my fucked-up family in San Francisco would be any less fucked up than it ever is?' I'm pretty sure work is his escape."

"Yeah well, Savage doesn't like or trust people he doesn't know well. He barely trusts you. Let's keep Dexter being here on the down-low."

"Fuck," Lucifer curses suddenly.

"Hey man," I say. "It sucks, but it's his honeymoon."

"I don't give two flips about Dexter and Savage. We have facial recognition on Max." He's already standing, shoving his computer into his bag. "Rooftop. Two buildings down."

I curse, and stick the binoculars to my face, spotting him and the glint of a rifle. "He's got a gun," I say, dropping the binoculars to my chest. I'm already running. "I'm going after Rick and Candace."

Lucifer pulls his weapons. "I'll cover you and send Dexter after Max."

Savage

We eat our ice cream inside the ice cream parlor, and when we exit to the street, Candace grabs my arm. "Candy." She points to a candy store. "For later. We can take it home."

"Not yes, but hell yes," I say. "Let's go." I grab her hand and we start a fast walk, nearing a jog.

A car passes, and I pull her along, running across the street and down a block. She's laughing as we walk into the store. "You are crazy. I say 'Candy' and we're literally running for the goods like it's a treasure."

"Exactly," I say, giving her a wink and heading for the display cases of chocolate. Five minutes later, I've had the counter clerk bag about a hundred dollars' worth of every chocolate they sell. That includes an elderberry truffle, whatever the fuck that is. We're just about to pay when Candace spies the cotton candy.

"I'm stuffed, but I have to have it," she says. "It's been forever and it's even pink. I wonder what the pink tastes like."

"Sugar," I promise. "Sticky sugar." I lean in close. "I'll lick it off for you when we get home."

She grins. "Promise?"

With that response, I decide it's time to head back to the room.

I pay for the sweets and once we're outside, I motion to a bench where we can eat and I can call for a car. "No signal," I say, standing up and walking a few steps. Right about the time I get a signal, I pause with a rush of unease. My gaze lifts and out of nowhere it seems, Adam is running toward Candace. At the same instant, the crack of gunshots pierces the air. One, two, they keep coming.

CHAPTER THIRTY-NINE

Savage

It's as if everything is in slow motion.

Adam and Candace go down and I see blood. There's more gunfire, but it's not coming from the same weapon, rather multiples weapons but I can't see the shooters. I react, doing all I can do with no target. And at this point, all I can do is what I do. I run for Adam and Candace and throw myself over the top of both of them. Adam groans beneath me and I can hear Candace murmuring, "Oh God. Oh God, oh God, oh God."

More like *Mother of God, help me save them.* More bullets crack in the air, pinging from multiple locations, but nothing flies in our direction or hits me. I give it thirty seconds, and since I'd like to live another day, and for Candace and Adam to do the same, I know I need to get us under cover. I pull my weapon, roll off of Adam and scan my surroundings to find no obvious threat. Adam, in turn, rolls to his back, his arm pouring blood. "Tell me she's okay."

I'm already leaning over Candace.

"My arm," she whispers. "It's my arm."

I rip open her sleeve, relieved to find what turns out to be a surface wound that will hurt and bleed like a bitch, and require stitches, but it's not going to cause permanent damage. Adam got her out of the line of fire and saved her damn life. "You're okay, baby. It's just a deep gash. It took some flesh, but you're okay." I pull off my shirt, rip it and tie her arm off to stop the bleeding before I do a body check for any other injury. Once I know she's clear I move to Adam's side and get right to work on his arm.

"How is she?" he asks.

"Flesh wound thanks to you, my man." I shove his sleeve up his arm.

"Good," he says, grimacing and trying to see his arm. "How bad?" he asks softly, and just the question tells me he knows it's not good.

He's bleeding like a stuck pig and stopping that flow now is critical. I begin the tourniquet process while gunfire echoes from several blocks down.

"Damn it, *how bad,* Savage?" Adam repeats, his face pinched in pain.

"A lot better than if you get shot again because we're sitting out in the open. Are you hit anywhere else?"

"No," he bites out. "Just my arm."

But that's just it. It's never *just* an arm. Ninety percent of all soldiers who die of bullet wounds in the field were hit in the arm, in a major artery. Details a doctor doesn't share with a man with a bullet in his arm. I finish the tourniquet and say, "We need to move."

Adam, the badass that he is, pushes himself upward and to his feet, sticky blood all down his side. The good news is if he'd hit a major artery, he'd be dead or close to it right now, not standing. But he's bleeding too much. He needs my attention.

Everyone on the street has taken cover, but a brave, short, and stubby middle-aged man rushes out of an office and to our sides. "We need to get you under cover," he proclaims. "My medical office is right here." He motions over his shoulder. "I called an ambulance, but they're really slow-going around these parts. I can try to help."

I don't argue. What he can do to help is provide shelter and the supplies I need to save Adam. I'll do the rest.

I scoop Candace up and head for the office. "Please tell me Adam's going to be okay," Candace says, pain radiating in her voice, but she's lucid and safe. That's at least one of the two of them.

"He's got me," I say, and while yes, I'm confident in my skills, I want her to be right now as well. "He'll be just fine."

I open the office door to what turns out to be a veterinarian's office not a doctor's office, but I'll make it work. Just behind the reception area, I find exactly what I need: an operating room with three tables long enough to hold a human. I lay Candace down on one of them, grab a couple of pillows from a chair nearby and prop up her arm. "Keep it above your heart. I'll stitch it up once Adam's stable." I pull my phone out, punch in Lucifer's number, and press it into her hand. "Make sure we're clear."

I don't wait for an answer. I rush into the lobby to find Adam leaning against the wall. "I'm trying not to bleed on his floor."

"It washes," the vet says dismissively. "And it's seen worse than blood, believe you me."

I grab Adam and hold onto him, eyeing the vet. "I'm a licensed surgeon," I say. "I need to get the bullet out and sew him up. I need tools. Whatever you can get me. I don't need much. Just the basics." It's not a question and I'm already walking Adam into the back room. Once he's on a table, he sits. I lay him down and get his arm elevated.

Glancing over my shoulder at Candace, I can see her talking on the phone and I'm eager to know what the hell is going on.

"There's a local sedative," the vet, whatever his name is, informs me, rolling a tray to my side. "And a sedative calculated for a human dosage."

"Numb my wife," I order, while Candace calls out, "Lucifer says Max is in sight, fleeing town."

In other words, Max isn't about to walk in and start shooting. That news alone eases the pressure of the moment, but it's not enough. And while I know Candace is hurting, she won't be for long, and right now I have no choice but to use her. "Call Blake, baby," I say, unwrapping Adam's arm and trying to control the bleeding to assess the damage. "Tell him what happened. Have him call the locals and control the situation."

Thank fuck for the supplies I now have at my disposal. I focus on clamping off a vein, and then try to find the bullet.

By the time I'm done, Candace calls out. "Blake is on it. Apparently, Dexter is here helping Lucifer."

I scowl and Adam says, "I knew he was here. Be glad he is." He grunts in pain.

I grab the sedative. "Time to go to sleep."

He lifts his head. "No sedative. I can't be knocked out when—"

I shove the needle into his arm and he growls. "Bastard!" and relaxes against the table.

The vet—I still don't know his name—chuckles. "He should be glad you made that decision for him. I got Candace numbed up."

"Feel better, baby?" I call out.

"Better," she confirms. "Yes."

At that moment, I can hear the front door open, and then a shout of "EMS!"

"I've got this," the vet says, rushing away.

Sixty seconds later, an EMS tech, a tall, bald fucker so white he glows, is standing across from me. I pull the bullet from Adam's arm, drop it in in a tray, and spurt out my credentials, before I say, "Check my wife. Take her vitals and make sure she's got enough pressure on that arm to stop the bleeding. She's not going with you. He is. I don't think he has arterial damage but without the right equipment, I can't be sure."

The tech just blinks.

"Move," I snap.

He jolts into action.

Another EMS tech steps in front of me, a redhead with a ruddy glow about him. "What can I do?"

"Check his vitals," I say. "I didn't exactly have time to do this right."

"Police," someone shouts from behind me, in the doorway. "Rick Savage?"

"A little fucking busy right now!" I call out.

The man in blue steps across from me next to the tech who's already checking Adam's blood pressure. "It's low," he announces.

I glance at the reading. "He's fine." I eye the cop. "What?"

"We've put out an APB on Max Bryant. He won't get far."

"No," I say tightly. "He won't."

I finish the last stitch needed in Adam's arm and step back, eyeing the EMS tech. "Get him to the hospital and tell them to scan for arterial damage." I back up and step next to Candace, as the other EMS tech tightens a bandage around her arm. "How are you, baby?"

"He says it's not that bad," she murmurs. "And I'm numb now, so it doesn't hurt, but I feel shaky."

"Adrenaline from the drugs and shock," I say, glancing at the tech, with a silent question.

"I can't move my fingers," she says, sounding slightly panicked. "Is that normal?"

I settle my hand on her head. "It's the numbing agent, baby. You'll be good as new soon."

"You're sure?" she asks, moving her fingers slightly. "I think I'm moving my fingers. I am, right?"

My lips curve at the control freak in her that has to solve this problem right this minute. "Yes," I assure her. "You are."

"She was lucky," the tech interjects. "She needs antibiotics and stitches and she'll be good as new. You sure you don't want her to go to the hospital?"

"No hospital," I confirm, not about to put her in a public place where Max can get to her. He tried to kill her. I'm not giving him a second chance to make that happen.

The tech gives a nod and steps away, helping to roll Adam out of the room.

About the same time, our vet with the "medical office" steps to my side. "What can I do?" he asks.

The dude is nothing if not generous with his aid. I reach into my pocket, pull out my wallet, and offer him a few large bills. He waves them off and says, "What else can I do to help?"

I shove the money into my pocket. "Supplies to stitch her up when I get her someplace safe, with a stock of pain meds and antibiotics."

"You got it. What else?"

"You aren't going to ask what this is all about?"

"And ruin a chance to hear all the town speculation and gossip with full interest? How boring would that be?"

It's an answer I respect. "The name is Rick Savage. You need a favor, you find me. New York City."

"Joe Montgomery," he says, shaking my hand. "Ex-military myself, son. If you ever need me again, you know where to find me."

I don't ask how he knows I'm ex-military. There were plenty of clues and he's clearly not a dumb man. I give him a nod, call a car, and when I would carry Candace, she waves me off. "I'll walk."

I help her to her feet, hold her to my side to keep her steady. Joe hands me the supplies, and I guide Candace to the door, dropping the cash on the front desk. I used his supplies. I'm not making him eat those expenses. Once I get Candace into the car, I direct the driver to take us to the hotel. Not my first choice, but Max isn't hunting us right now. He's being hunted. And the hotel is a quick shelter and a place my team can find me.

The minute we're in the backseat, I turn to Candace and cup her face. I open my mouth to speak, but nothing comes out. I don't even know what to say to her right now. She almost died today and so did Adam. Because of me.

CHAPTER FORTY

Savage

I kiss Candace hard and fast, the taste of her on my lips sweet, the only thing sweet about me. She's my opposite, right where I'm wrong. Light where I'm dark. Too good for me and yet exactly what I need. And I don't know what to do with that on a night like this one. I pull back, but she catches my hand.

"This wasn't your fault. I see that in your eyes, Rick Savage. The blame, so much blame. You need to stop. It's not good for us. It's not good for you."

My lips press together. "It's the truth."

"It's *not* the truth."

My cellphone rings. She inhales and releases me, turning away, obviously aware that I need to take just about any call headed in my direction right now. In this case, it's Blake.

"Yeah, boss," I answer. "What's up?"

"A fuck show, from what I hear. How's Candace?"

"She needs stitches, pain meds, and antibiotics, but she's alive."

"And Adam? She told me he was hit pretty bad."

"I knocked him out, pulled out the bullet, and stitched him up, but he was bleeding like a motherfucker. I had EMS take him in for a scan. He'll be pissed as shit but alive." I pause. "He saved her life. No fucking doubt about it. Any word from Lucifer?"

"He warned me he was going silent. He's on Max's trail. He'll find him. He'll bring him in and Max will go to jail for this. Let him and me handle this."

"Fuck jail for Max. That's *not* how this ends. Pull your people back."

"Don't go down the bullshit path, Savage. My people are your people."

"Not if that's how you think this ends. Consider this my resignation. I'm done, Blake." I hang up.

"What just happened?" Candace demands, grabbing my arm. "Rick, what just happened?"

"What was necessary," I say tightly. "I didn't belong with Walker anyway. My ways are not their ways."

"You know that's not true," she says. "You're responding to and with anger."

"Damn straight," I confirm and my phone starts ringing again.

Of course, it's Blake again, and I decline the call and ignore the buzz of text messages that follow. I dial Lucifer. He doesn't answer. I leave him a message. "I need to talk to you now. Call me."

The car halts in front of the hotel. I slide my phone into my pocket and concentrate on what matters right now. Taking care of Candace. Revenge and retribution will come next.

I help her out of the car and wrap my arm around her, holding her close. I obviously didn't do that well enough earlier today. I walked away from her. I had a gut feeling and I still walked away.

Once we're on the elevator, Candace says, "Don't let this take you to a bad place, Rick."

"If me making the person who did this pay is me in a bad place, we have a problem. I never promised to be anything but who I am. And this is who I am, Candace."

The elevator halts. I catch her hand and walk her to me, staring down at her. "You know I have to—"

"That's just it," she says. "I *do* know. I know you. I know what you intend to do. *I know*. I just don't want you to get in trouble."

"I know how to do what I do. You need to trust me." That's where I leave the conversation. The elevator doors open and I wrap my arm around her and guide her out of the car and into the hallway, steadying her and sheltering her every way I can. It's all too little, too late, and I know that, too. I won't make that mistake again. Nothing she says is going to change my mind about what comes next. Max is as good as dead.

Once we're inside the room, I hold up a hand and have her wait just inside the door while I ensure we're secure. When I'm comfortable we're safe, I have her sit on a lounge chair, prop pillows beneath her, and then grab towels, hot water, my own medical bag, and the vet's supplies and go down on a knee beside her. With her arm on top of towels and propped on the armrest, I grab the numbing agent. "I'm going to put some extra in to make sure you don't feel the stitches."

She nods and I get to work.

She's tough, and way too quiet through the entire process, but then, she's coming down off a hell of a rush of adrenaline.

Fifteen minutes later, she's stitched up, and I'm comfortable with how she'll heal. "You rest," I say. "I'm going to call and check on Adam."

Instead of resting, she shifts to a full sitting position, reaching for her purse at her hip, and struggling to open it as she asks, "Should I try Lucifer?"

I walk to the chair beside her, sit down and reach over her, pulling her phone from her purse. Since I've made sure she has every Walker number under the sun in her phone, it's not hard to location Lucifer's number. I press the phone into her hand, tension crackling between us, which does nothing to mute how damn in love we are.

"Yes," I say because I know Candace. Actively working toward a solution helps her feel she has some semblance of control. "Call him," I add, punching the call button for her and standing up to dial the hospital.

While I wait for someone to track down info on my "brother" Adam, Candace gives a shake of her head, silently telling me that Lucifer isn't answering. *Bastard.* Meanwhile, on my end, a woman comes back on the line for me. "I'm still trying to get you to the right place. Hold just a little bit longer." She doesn't wait for my agreement. She puts me back on hold. Another five minutes and I'm forced to leave my number.

Candace is now sitting on the edge of the couch. She's pale, a troubled expression on her face. I slide my phone into my pocket. "You okay, baby?"

"Is he—is Adam dead?"

"No," I say, closing the space between us and going down on one knee in front of her. "No, he's not dead. I only sent him for a scan to be safe. If we were out in the field on a mission, we wouldn't have the luxury."

"I'm still scared for him."

"I know," I say, and my hands come down on her knees. My voice lowers, rasps with guilt, and the magnitude of all that's just happened. "Baby, I'm sorry this happened. I'm so damn sorry."

"There you go again," she accuses. "Blaming yourself. Stop blaming yourself. *Please*, I *beg of you*."

"I'm the one who decided to help Max. Me. I did it."

"You already told me you aren't sure you could have walked away. There's more to this than either of us know yet."

"It's all about my life, my choices, my past. I did this." I stand up on an explosion of anger, and guilt, tormented now as I add, "This is why I stayed away. This is why I knew I couldn't marry you."

She is instantly on her feet. "Really, Rick?" she demands. "*That's* where you're going? You shouldn't *be here*? You shouldn't have married me? Thirty seconds after we got married?" She presses her good arm under her bad arm, in front of her body, and tears explode from her eyes. She's sobbing, but she's angry, shouting at me, "These tears do not make me weak. These are tears of acceptance. You will *always* hurt me. You aren't capable of just loving me, so don't worry. We'll annul the marriage and you can just leave me alone for good this time. I'm done. I'm so done."

That proclamation is a blade through my heart a hundred times. I step into her, hands on her shoulders. "You are not done. We are *not* done. I don't want an annulment."

"I heard what you said, Rick. You shouldn't have married me."

"I said this is why I didn't in the past. But I know what happened when I left you. They still came for you. I'm just trying to figure out how to protect you."

"By being with me."

"I'm not suggesting anything else."

"Aren't you?" she challenges. "I *can't* do this back and forth. I can't. I love you too much. You have too much ability to hurt me. And I let that happen all over again."

There's a knock on the door, which could mean any number of things good or bad, but right now, I'm not quite ready to let go of Candace.

"I know I hurt you in the past, Candace. That's not where this is going."

"You said—"

"Look beneath the words and you will see that there is one theme. I can't lose you, Candace. I thought I lost you today and it killed me. I love you so fucking much." The knock sounds again.

"I love you, too, but you are just gutting me, Rick. And just—damn it, you have to get the door."

I force myself to step back and I pull my weapon. "This conversation isn't over and neither are we."

I head for the door.

LISA RENEE JONES

CHAPTER FORTY-ONE

Savage

I pause at the door and call out, "Who is it?"

"Adam, you fucker."

"What the hell?" I murmur, yanking open the door to find him leaning on the doorjamb, looking pale as a bloodsucker.

"Yeah. What the hell?" he demands.

"Holy fuck, man." I shove my gun in my pants, back up, and let him enter. "How are you here? Did you get scanned?"

"Apparently," he says dryly, walking past me.

I scowl at his back. "What does apparently mean?" I call after him, shutting the door and locking it before following him into the living room.

At which point, Candace runs to him and hugs him with her one good arm. "Oh God," she exclaims. "Thank God. You're okay."

He pats her back with his one good hand. "Now, now, you're going to make your husband jealous and I need to slink my Jell-O legs to the couch."

The use of the word "husband" punches me in the gut. I *am* her husband. I don't intend for that to change, but I just fucked up with Candace. Over and over, I keep fucking up with Candace.

Adam extracts himself from her hold and manages to round the coffee table before he pretty much thuds to the couch. I step to the opposite side of the coffee table. "What does apparently mean, Adam?" I press.

"I woke up as they pulled me out of the damn machine." He eyes Candace. "You sure you're okay?"

"I'm fine," she says, sitting on the chair to my left and studying him. "I'm not sure we can say the same about you."

I couldn't agree more, I think, which is exactly why I say, "You're here way too fast. I knocked you out."

He smirks. "I handle my drugs and booze well, remember?"

I grimace. "You said you took the scan. Did you see a doctor?"

"That would be you, my doctor, so yes, I did."

"What the hell, Adam?" I repeat.

"Chill out, man. I convinced the tech, despite some stupid rule he couldn't tell me I'm fine, to tell me I'm fine."

I don't ask how Adam got the tech who isn't supposed to give him results to tell him his results. The same way I would have: any way I had to.

"Therefore," he continues, "I left and here I am, here in the nick of time, before you go and do something stupid."

Before I can comment on that dastardly remark, Candace takes over. "I think you need to go back to the hospital. You don't look good, Adam."

"Not happening. Besides," he motions to me, "I had one of the best fucking surgeons on planet Earth fix me in a vet's office. I'm golden."

There's another knock on the door. Adam and I exchange a concerned look. Wordlessly, I head back to the door, pulling my gun as I once again call out, "Who is it?"

"Lucifer," comes the reply.

Which means he's not with Max. Damn it to hell. I jerk the door open and back up. "He got away," I accuse.

"Of course not, man," he assures me, stepping into the room. "Dexter tracked him to a cabin just outside town."

"Yeah," I say. "About that. How the hell is Dexter here and I didn't know?"

"Interesting story that worked out in our favor. How's Adam?" He doesn't explain the story or wait for a reply. He heads into the living room, clearly aware that Adam's here, which means Adam already knew where Max was before Lucifer got here.

I'm glad I saved his ass so I can beat it.

I shove the gun back in my pants and I hear Lucifer say, "Ah shit, man. Adam. How the fuck are you?"

"Alive," Adam says. "That's about as good as it gets."

I step back into the room and scowl at Adam. "Start talking."

He holds up his good hand. "Before you go all ape shit crazy on me, you should know that Lucifer knew there was a shooter before anyone. He's the only reason I had a chance to do what I did."

"Then Lucifer," I say, stepping next to him, "is a rockstar and I owe him, but we're not talking about Lucifer." I look between the two of them. "Why is Dexter here?"

"He has family in San Francisco," Adam explains. "And as family does to each other, they pissed him off. He wanted an excuse to escape them and luckily, he came over here right about the time Max started shooting."

"Such perfect timing," I say. A little too perfect.

"He's cool, man," Lucifer assures me. "I'm telling you. Dex isn't dirty."

I said the same thing about Max, but I don't point that out. There's no point. "I need that location for Max," I say, "and then all of you, Dexter included, are done here."

Adam snorts. "That's not happening."

"I left Walker," I say. "This is a me issue now. I'm going to handle Max."

"Because you need no one?" Adam asks, shoving to his feet. "Because the way I see it, if you head off to kill Max, you have to leave Candace alone. Is that really what you want?"

"I already planned on your wounded ass staying with Candace," I snap. I glance at Lucifer. "Protect your job. Get out of this while you can."

"According to Blake when I talked to him about five minutes ago, and I quote 'help him, no matter what that means.' And he said to tell you, resignation not accepted."

"Fuck him."

"He said to tell you fuck you, too," Lucifer replies.

Candace laughs. My head cuts in her direction. "You laughed."

"It was worthy of a laugh and since I was just shot, really, *really* worthy. Take Lucifer with you and go do what you have to do. And come back to me."

I close the space between me and her, and I don't care who's watching. My hand slides under her hair, and I lean close. "Candace—"

"I'm not going anywhere. And neither are you. But we're going to talk about what just happened. Loudly, most likely." Her fingers curl on my shirt. "Come back to me and do so whole."

"I will, baby." I kiss her and not gently. "I love you."

"I love you, too."

Reluctantly, I release her and turn to Adam. "Protect her."

He indicates his arm and says, "With my life, man."

I give him a slow deep nod that says I trust him, and it's a thank you. He nods and I turn to Lucifer. "Let's go."

CHAPTER FORTY-TWO

Savage

Lucifer leads me to a moonlit hilltop a good ten miles south of downtown Sonoma. We locate Dexter, behind a cluster of trees, where Dexter is belly flat on the ground with a pair of binoculars. I get low with him. Lucifer comes in on the other side of me. "Talk to me."

"He's been sitting in front of his computer eating potato chips for the last fifteen minutes." He hands me the binoculars. "He's on bag two."

I accept the lenses and take a gander at the view and I don't know what it is about hillbilly-ass cabins Max likes, but he's hiding out in yet another one. Homing in on the window view, sure enough, Max, the potato chip-eating bastard, is stuffing his face. That little prick shot my woman and best friend, and then went on back to the ol' cabin to stuff his ugly face. I hand off the lenses to Lucifer and side-eye Dexter. "You sure he's alone?"

"Positive," he responds. "I covered the house twice over and I've been sitting here damn near two hours."

And he's still alive. He's full of shit. There's a reason Max is sitting there eating potato chips. He booby-trapped the hell out of this place. "He's been at that computer all this time?" I ask.

"He spent a shit ton of time cleaning his guns."

That actually sounds like Max. He's obsessed with cleaning his guns, especially after a kill. He might just think Candace and/or Adam are dead. But right now, I want to know who's at my back. "How did you get here just in time?"

"I'd say luck, but I can't really call my sister being a bitch good luck. I guess for once, she was a well-timed bitch. And don't even get me started on her bitch-ass boyfriend who's lucky to be alive right now, with his investment banking tips and bullshit attitude about 'anyone not like me.' And don't ask what that means. I might go shoot that fucker in that stupid-ass cabin for you. Want me to?"

"I got it," I say. "But don't make yourself next." With that, I don't check in with Lucifer. I just start moving.

"Wait," Dexter growls. "Just wait."

I pause and glare at him. "What?"

"He's got the place booby-trapped out the ass." He points in front of him. "Straight line down to the house."

"Why don't you lead the way?"

"Yeah. Sure. Whatever."

He shifts to a squat and then starts moving. Lucifer eases closer to me. "Told you to trust him."

"I'm nowhere near trust at this point," I say, "but you go right ahead."

He laughs and accepts my invitation, easing behind Dexter.

I go the other direction, well aware of how Max operates. I pull a flashlight from my pocket and head around back, following the lines of the trees where he loves to play dirty. I sidestep several potential traps and then I'm at the backdoor. I pull my weapon, kick in the door, and I'm blasting through the tiny cabin. Max has his guard down. He's left with a computer and an empty bag of potato chips as his weapons.

He curses and stands up, but I fire a round to his left and right and at his feet, and I'm on top of him before he can act. I flatten him on the ground, plant my boot on his chest, and my weapon at his neck. The front door bursts open and Lucifer barges into the cabin.

I'm aware of him, but I don't care about him, not right now. "Why, Max?"

Max laughs a bitter laugh. "*Why*? You moved the insurance. You fucked me. I had a sweet payout and you fucked it up."

"I didn't move shit. I just never put it where you thought I did. And what happened to all your money?"

"I needed the money," he groans. "That's all you need to know."

"Obviously your old enemy story was bullshit. Who was paying you?"

"I'm not telling you shit."

"I will shoot your fingers off one by one. And this is me saying this. You know I don't bluff."

Dexter appears beside Max, his possible ally and I'm about two seconds from shooting his ass when he grabs Max's hand, holds it down, and steps on it. A crunching sound follows Max's groan of, "Bastard."

Dexter smirks. There is definitely a side to him I do not know. I'm not sure if I love him or hate him.

Max is another story. I hate his fucking ass. I glare at him. "Talk"

Dexter grinds Max's hand.

Wuss-ass Max gives up the goods. "A guy name Mick North wanted the goods on Allen," Max snarls.

"The former NSA director," I say and this is all starting to make sense to me.

"Yeah, fucktard," he says, using my word which gets him no points. "Who else do you think I mean?"

Lucifer pulls out his computer and sits down at the table. "I'm looking him up."

"Mick was going to pay me big," Max continues. "But he had eyes on both of us. He followed you. He got the drive in Nashville before I ever knew where you hid it. He was watching you. You aren't as good as you think."

"And he tried to get rid of you after he had it," I assume. "That's why he came at you at the cabin."

"Yeah. It could have ended there but when he found out there was nothing in your little insurance holes, he thought I double-crossed him. He found where I was hiding my wife. He *killed her*. So, *I* killed him, and I made it hurt, but it wasn't enough. You did this to me. Your wife needs to die. I hope she's dead."

That's all I need to hear. I shoot him between the eyes.

"Well, that was kind of anticlimactic," Dexter comments.

"No, it's not," Lucifer says. "Because we're not done yet. Mick isn't a nobody. He's ex-CIA. His file is classified. Blake's overriding the system. We're looking for a photo and location for Mick." He keys a few more strokes and says, "Got it. And oh shit." He glances up at me. "It's the investor from the museum."

"Kirk Long?" I ask, this whole big picture coming together and not in a good way.

"Well, that's the thing," Lucifer says. "Mick looks a whole lot like Kirk. He seems to have assumed his identity." He motions me forward and I move in behind him to peer at his computer. He enlarges a photo of each man. He's right. They look alike but they aren't the same person.

"Where's the real Kirk Long?" I ask.

"I'm guessing he's dead and Mick claimed his money, but Blake is working on that angle."

Dexter joins us and eyes the photos. "I don't know where Kirk is, but Mick's in the other room, on the bed. He's dead to the world tired."

I eye him and decide any stupid joke told by someone else is just that: stupid. I walk to the single bedroom in the place, and Dexter wasn't lying. Mick is dead, flat on his back on the bed, and ironically, considering how I killed Max, he has a bullet between his eyes. I walk back into the main cabin. "That's Mick or Kirk, or whoever the asshole really is."

Lucifer bags his computer. "I just heard from Blake. The real Kirk is on sabbatical in Europe. He told his staff and family he'd be off-grid for a month two weeks ago."

"In other words, he's dead," I supply.

"Most likely," Lucifer agrees. "We'll know more soon. Blake said to tell you to go be with your wife. We'll clean this up." He tosses me the keys. "We have a ride coming."

I don't argue. I catch the keys and head for the door.

Five minutes later, I'm behind the wheel. Twenty minutes later, I'm at the hotel. I walk into the room and I expect Candace and Adam to be knocked out. The minute I open the door, Candace is in front of me. "What happened?"

"Where's Adam?"

"Asleep. Rick, what happened?"

"He's dead. I'll explain it all later." I drag her to me and cup her face. "I'm sorry. I can handle a lot of things, but seeing you down with blood all over you, it fucked with me. I was not in a good place."

"I know and that's why I calmed down, but don't go there again."

"Never, baby. No matter what. You are everything to me. *Everything.*"

"The answer can't be that you leave me again."

"I was never going to leave you. God, woman, I can't lose you. That's the bottom line. And I will do a better job of protecting you."

"You expect too much of yourself. I just need you, but we're all in or not at all."

"Baby, I have always been all in with you. You are my best friend. You are my *wife*. My life. *Forever.*"

"Don't forget that," she whispers.

"I haven't forgotten anything about you and me since the moment I met you." I stroke her hair behind her ear. "What do you say, when you and Adam are well enough to leave, we pack up and go to the Hamptons and look for that land to build our forever home?"

"I'd like that, Rick. So much."

LISA RENEE JONES

CHAPTER FORTY-THREE

Candace

One month later...

I'm at the coffee pot in the kitchen of the gorgeous Hamptons house Rick and I have been staying at the past few weeks while looking for land. Rick thought it would give us a chance to just be us, an extended honeymoon, and it's turned out to be wonderful.

Rick appears in the doorway in nothing but his beach trunks, all those muscles of his on display, which is just fine by me. I smile a tiny smile at the amended tattoo on his chest that no longer just says "San Antonio." It now has my name underneath it.

"I'm keeping you even if you kick me to curb," he'd joked as he'd surprised me with his new ink, but I'd gone all-in as well. A few days later, his tattoo artist had snuck me on his schedule. I'd surprised Rick and gotten my first tattoo ever. A heart with "Savage" in the center on the inside of my wrist. I told him I'd chosen "Savage" rather than "Rick" because every girl wants a Savage in her life, well, at least in some way. He'd just laughed.

"Come, my love," he purrs, curling his fingers in my direction. "I have a surprise for you."

I set my coffee cup down and close the space between us, wrapping my arms around him. "Once again. I'm just telling you in advance, I'm not having sex on the porch in the broad daylight."

"We'll wait until dusk then," he teases, kissing me and then turning me toward the front door.

He opens it and urges me outside and the minute I step on the porch, I immediately start laughing. There are now two white wooden rockers to my left. He steps behind me, his hands on my shoulder. "So we can grow old together and sit on our very own porch, once it's built, in our rockers. Try yours out."

I claim one of the chairs and his cellphone rings. He snags it from his pocket and glances at the caller ID. "Blake," he informs me and then answers with, "Two months, Blake. I'm not coming back sooner." He listens a minute and says, "Alrighty then. I've heard it all. I'll tell her." He disconnects and sits down. "They found the real Kirk."

I blink in surprise. "As in alive?"

"Yep. He was at some Buddhist camp, as in a real sabbatical. He had no idea his identity and money had been stolen, but turns out he's so rich and so well protected that what Mick took was a drop in the bucket. And he feels so bad about the museum deal, that he offered to fund the project."

"Well, that's good," I say. "But I think the past is the past. I'll leave that project behind. I have a house to think about."

His lips curve. "Yes, you do." He starts rocking and does his best old man voice. "You know, honey, my back hurts. I think it would feel better if we were in the bed with no clothes on."

I laugh. "You're crazy."

"I'm serious." He stands up, picks me up, and carries me in the house, where there is no doubt he will try to get me naked. And I'll let him.

THE END

Thank you so much for joining me Savage's finale! I am going to miss this ridiculous, insane, sweet alpha something fierce! Want more Walker Security? Check out Adrian's Trilogy! It's complete and available everywhere!

SAVAGE ENDING

https://www.lisareneejones.com/walker-security-adrians-trilogy.html

---

If you loved the other Walker Security men, check out the other series from that world: Tall, Dark, and Deadly (Royce's, Luke's, and Blake's stories) and Walker Security (Kyle's, Asher's, and Jacob's stories)!

What's next from me? THE NECKLACE TRILOGY!

In the vein of her Inside Out series, New York Times Bestselling Author Lisa Renee Jones returns

with the dark, seductive world of the Necklace Trilogy...

Allison Wright is delivered a package meant for a different Allison—a unique, expensive necklace. Determined to right the confusion, she seeks out the proper recipient, a journey that takes her to the doorstep of Tyler Hawk, a good looking, recluse billionaire who deals with fine collectibles such as the necklace. She also learns that Allison, his employee, quit her job registering and restoring his vast assortment of collectibles. Ironically, Allison is the daughter of a rather famous archeologist who is also employed by a local museum, and her love of such things has her jumping at the opportunity. Soon she is spending her evening and weekends immersed in the job the other Allison left behind.

As Allison begins diving into the job for Tyler, secrets about the other Allison begin to surface that have her concerned for her safety. And as she starts hunting for answers, her path crosses with the enigmatic famous author who has a business endeavor with her boss. Dash Black is a man who is dark and edgy, intense and yet quiet. Funny and yet somehow reserved. He draws her in, sets her pulse racing, and her body on fire. She knows there's a dangerous edge to him, but she can't seem to care. She's addicted to everything he is and she simply can't turn away, no matter what the cost. As Allison is drawn into the life and mystery of the other Allison, a mystery demands answers and passion burns hot. Allison will travel a path that leads to shocking truths and a side of herself she never knew existed.

PRE-ORDER AND LEARN MORE HERE:

https://www.lisareneejones.com/necklace-trilogy.html

Don't forget, if you want to be the first to know about upcoming books, giveaways, sales and any other exciting news I have to share please be sure you're signed up for my newsletter! As an added bonus everyone receives a free ebook when they sign-up!

http://lisareneejones.com/newsletter-sign-up/

EXCERPT FROM THE WALKER SECURITY: ADRIAN TRILOGY

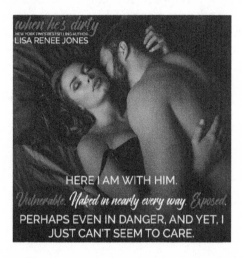

when he's dirty

NEW YORK TIMES BESTSELLING AUTHOR
LISA RENEE JONES

HERE I AM WITH HIM.
Vulnerable. Naked in nearly every way. Exposed.
PERHAPS EVEN IN DANGER, AND YET, I
JUST CAN'T SEEM TO CARE.

I exit the bathroom and halt to find him standing in the doorway, his hands on either side of the doorframe. "What are you doing?

"This," he says, and suddenly, his hands are on my waist, and he's walked me back into the bathroom.

Before I know what's happening, he's kicked the door shut, and his fingers are diving into my hair. "Kissing you, because I can't fucking help myself. And because you might not ever let me do it again. That is unless you object?"

That's the part that really gets me. The "unless I object," the way he manages to be all alpha and demanding and still ask. Well, and the part where he can't fucking help himself.

I press to my toes and the minute my mouth meets his, his crashes over mine, his tongue doing a wicked lick that I feel in every part of me. And I don't know what I taste like to him, but he is temptation with a hint of tequila, demand, and desire. His hands slide up my back, fingers splayed between my shoulder blades, his hard body pressed to mine, seducing me in every possible way.

I moan with the feel of him and his lips part from mine, lingering there a moment before he says, "Obviously, someone needs to protect you from me," he says. "Like me." And then to my shock, he releases me and leaves. The bathroom door is open and closed before I know what's happened. And once again, I have no idea if or when I will ever see him again.

FIND OUT MORE ABOUT THE ADRIAN TRILOGY HERE:

https://www.lisareneejones.com/walker-security-adrians-trilogy.html

THE BRILLIANCE TRILOGY

It all started with a note, just a simple note handwritten by a woman I didn't know, never even met. But in that note is perhaps every answer to every question I've ever had in my life. And because of that note, I look for her but find him. I'm drawn to his passion, his talent, a darkness in him that somehow becomes my light, my life. Kace August is rich, powerful, a rock star of violins, a man who is all tattoos, leather, good looks, and talent. He has a wickedly sweet ability to play the violin, seducing audiences worldwide. Now, he's seducing me. I know he has secrets. I don't care. Because you see, I have secrets, too.

I'm not Aria Alard, as he believes. I'm Aria Stradivari, daughter to Alessandro Stradivari, a musician born from the same blood as the man who created the famous Stradivarius violin. I am as rare as the mere 650 instruments my ancestors created. Instruments worth millions. 650 masterpieces, the brilliance unmatched. 650 reasons to kill. 650 reasons to hide. One reason not to: him.

FIND OUT MORE ABOUT THE BRILLIANCE TRILOGY HERE:

https://www.lisareneejones.com/brilliance-trilogy.html

THE LILAH LOVE SERIES

As an FBI profiler, it's Lilah Love's job to think like a killer. And she is very good at her job. When a series of murders surface—the victims all stripped naked and shot in the head—Lilah's instincts tell her it's the work of an assassin, not a serial killer. But when the case takes her back to her hometown in the Hamptons and a mysterious but unmistakable connection to her own life, all her assumptions are shaken to the core.

Thrust into a troubled past she's tried to shut the door on, Lilah's back in the town where her father is mayor, her brother is police chief, and she has an intimate history with the local crime lord's son, Kane Mendez. The two share a devastating secret, and only Kane understands Lilah's own darkest impulses. As more corpses surface, so does a series of anonymous notes to Lilah, threatening to expose her. Is the killer someone in her own circle? And is she the next target?

FIND OUT MORE ABOUT THE LILAH LOVE SERIES HERE:

https://www.lisareneejonesthrillers.com/the-lilah-love-series.html

ALSO BY LISA RENEE JONES

THE INSIDE OUT SERIES

If I Were You
Being Me
Revealing Us
His Secrets*
Rebecca's Lost Journals
The Master Undone*
My Hunger*
No In Between
My Control*
I Belong to You
All of Me*

THE SECRET LIFE OF AMY BENSEN

Escaping Reality
Infinite Possibilities
Forsaken
Unbroken*

CARELESS WHISPERS

Denial
Demand
Surrender

WHITE LIES

Provocative
Shameless

TALL, DARK & DEADLY

Hot Secrets
Dangerous Secrets
Beneath the Secrets

WALKER SECURITY

Deep Under
Pulled Under
Falling Under

LILAH LOVE

Murder Notes
Murder Girl
Love Me Dead
Love Kills
Bloody Vows
Bloody Love (July 2021)

DIRTY RICH

Dirty Rich One Night Stand
Dirty Rich Cinderella Story
Dirty Rich Obsession
Dirty Rich Betrayal
Dirty Rich Cinderella Story: Ever After
Dirty Rich One Night Stand: Two Years Later
Dirty Rich Obsession: All Mine
Dirty Rich Secrets
Dirty Rich Betrayal: Love Me Forever

THE FILTHY TRILOGY

The Bastard
The Princess
The Empire

THE NAKED TRILOGY

One Man
One Woman
Two Together

THE SAVAGE SERIES

Savage Hunger
Savage Burn
Savage Love
Savage Ending

THE BRILLIANCE TRILOGY

A Reckless Note
A Wicked Song
A Sinful Encore

ADRIAN'S TRILOGY

When He's Dirty
When He's Bad
When He's Wild

NECKLACE TRILOGY

What If I Never? (October 2021)
Because I Can (December 2021)
When I Say Yes (February 2022)

*eBook only

ABOUT THE AUTHOR

New York Times and *USA Today* bestselling author Lisa Renee Jones writes dark, edgy fiction including the highly acclaimed *Inside Out* series and the crime thriller *The Poet*. Suzanne Todd (producer of Alice in Wonderland and Bad Moms) on the *Inside Out* series: *Lisa has created a beautiful, complicated, and sensual world that is filled with intrigue and suspense.*

Prior to publishing, Lisa owned a multi-state staffing agency that was recognized many times by The Austin Business Journal and also praised by the Dallas Women's Magazine. In 1998 Lisa was listed as the #7 growing women-owned business in Entrepreneur Magazine. She lives in Colorado with her husband, a cat that talks too much, and a Golden Retriever who is afraid of trash bags.

Made in the USA
Monee, IL
09 June 2021